The blue flame-tree

JEAN-LOUIS BAGHIO'O

THE BLUE FLAME-TREE

translated from the French by
Stephen Romer

with an afterword by
Maryse Condé

CARCANET PRESS · MANCHESTER

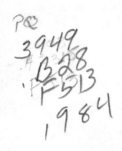

First published in Great Britain in 1984 by
Carcanet Press Ltd
208–212 Corn Exchange Buildings
Manchester M4 3BQ

Translation © Stephen Romer 1984

Le flamboyant à fleurs bleues was first published in 1973 by Calmann-Lévy; and
by Editions Caribéennes in 1981.

Baghio'o, Jean-Louis
  The blue flame-tree.
  I. Title   II. Le flamboyant à fleurs bleues
  English
  843'.914 [F]   PQ2603.A2315
  ISBN 0-85635-470-8

The publisher acknowledges the financial assistance of the Arts Council of Great Britain

Typeset by Paragon Photoset, Aylesbury
Printed in England by Short Run Press Ltd, Exeter

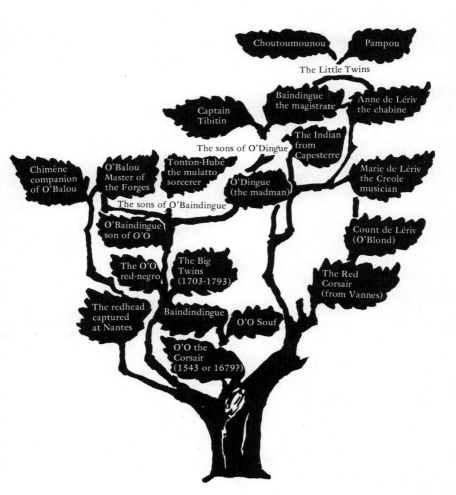

Choutoumounou   Pampou

The Little Twins

Baindingue
the magistrate

Anne de Lériv
the chabine

Captain
Tibitin

The Indian
from
Capesterre

The sons of O'Dingue

Chimène
companion
of O'Balou

O'Balou
Master of
the Forges

Tonton-Hubé
the mulatto
sorcerer

O'Dingue
(the madman)

Marie de Lériv
the Creole
musician

The sons of O'Baindingue

O'Baindingue
son of O'O

Count de Lériv
(O'Blond)

The O'O
red-negro

The Big
Twins
(1703-1793)

The Red
Corsair
(from Vannes)

The redhead
captured
at Nantes

Baindindingue

O'O Souf

O'O the
Corsair
(1543 or 1679?)

THE O'O FAMILY TREE

A ship from that fleet
Was wrecked not far from Athens, and without
The dolphins all would have met their end;
The animal's a trusty friend
To man.

La Fontaine, *Fables* IV,7

CHOUTOUMOUNOU, and his twin brother Pampou, came from a very old line of Guadeloupi slaves. They are well known in their village at Sainte-Anne. The founder of their family is a memory in the oral tradition, doubtless glorified by the shadowy charm of legend. Some would have it that a sloop manned by a crew of negroes and commanded by a bright-eyed giant with wide flaring nostrils and the kind of lips that press greedily upon the finer lips of women, pursued the slave-ships and freed their cargoes of 'ebony'.[1] The swift, skilfully handled ship, well stocked with arms, flew an unfamiliar flag: the skull and crossbones. This emblem soon became notorious, adopted by sea-roving pirates whose intention it was to lay the blame for their stealing and plundering on the negroes.

This 'chaser' was not authorized by any government. It operated independently, and hardly anyone involved in the slave-trade who saw it on the horizon managed to escape its volleys. French, English, Dutch and Spanish sailors who, by some miracle, evaded the usual massacre, recounted how the 'Monster' unleashed his men aboard their ships, crying 'O'O!...O'O!', and how a little long-haired negress who always fought by his side scythed off ears as they went, to thread into a necklace, and hummed in a soft caressing voice, as if in echo, 'O'O!...O'O!' — terrible syllables that increased the savagery of the demonic crew.

After the fight, the 'Capitaine' would have the captured white officers skinned alive. Then, during a diabolical ceremony in mid-ocean, the skins were dried out to make breeches, those famous

---

[1] The negroes.

corsair breeches, worn by the entire crew. So it was that, fighting bare-chested, they always appeared to be black and white.

It is hard to date these events. From the archives of the Spanish naval ministry one learns that a black pirate was prominent in the sack of Cartagena in 1543. The English and the French, oddly allied in this assault on a base belonging to Charles V, gave chase to the intruder. They didn't catch him, and he got away with a large part of the booty.

Some claim that it was at the second sack of Cartagena, instigated by Louis XIV in 1697, when an alliance was formed between a royal armada led by the Baron de Pointis and troops levied by the Governor of Casse from among the buccaneers and planters of San Domingo, that the black corsair or pirate was identified for the first time — but not captured. He joined the expedition, which is said to have come away with more than fifty million pounds, and made off with nearly ten million for himself. An ocean-wide search for the thief was mounted, but he disappeared wordlessly over the horizon.

Still others claim that O'O was none other than O'Makendal, the Mussulman from Guinea, who in 1758 was living in San Domingo. During a public meeting he dipped three handkerchiefs into an urn filled with the blood of a slave who had just had his throat slit like an animal. Extracting the first handkerchief which came out yellow he said: 'Here are the first inhabitants of the island'; then, soaking another handkerchief which came out white he said: 'Here are the present inhabitants'; finally, plunging his hand a third time into the famous urn, he brought out a black handkerchief and exclaimed, 'And here are they who will remain masters of the country! . . .' Upon which the subjugated negroes started a murderous revolt. Held responsible, O'Makendal was captured and broken on the wheel. His children, sold to the Dutch on the island of Saint-Martin, would finally have reappeared in Guadeloupe as the ancestors of Choutoumounou and Pampou.

History has it that Lord Houël, first governor of Guadeloupe, had worked fruitlessly for years trying to industrialize sugar production before he learned of a pair of negro twins on Saint-Martin who knew the secret of refining, the technique by which all traces of coloured matter are eliminated from the mild, sweet-tasting cane extract. The English had already mastered the blanching process and their business prospered. Now the Dutch were in the running, thanks to these two singular slaves. An avid Houël made enquiries. The twins appeared to be magicians of a kind; they were known to be very skilled at preparing skins in such a way as to prevent putrefaction and producing leather of such suppleness that it seemed like genuine chamois. In the process they made use of alum, salt and even fish oil. Apparently, they could also whiten Kio sugar — raw sugar — with certain plant extracts; but they would only pass on their secret to the Dutch in exchange for their freedom, that being the current bargain. Around 1641, Houël sent an expedition (a frequent enough procedure at that time) to capture what he so desired plus a whole Dutch ship loaded with slaves. This successful venture resulted in the French employing African labour, and made way for the real colonization of Guadeloupe.

In exchange for their secret, Houël promised the two industrious negroes their freedom. In full possession of their faculties, the twins accepted his terms. If slavery had been introduced simply to capture people whose knowledge was coveted, and then bargained for in this way, it might almost have been a fair game.

The two vigorous young men, tall and imposing, closely resembled one another. Their hair was curly rather than crinkly. With strange sea-green eyes they could maintain almost indefinite eye-to-eye contact, head and body still, without a single flicker, keeping an impenetrable silence. Despite an apprehensive, timid and rather distant air, they had a fiendish instinct for laying bare an ulterior motive. In Guadeloupe and Martinique the 'red-negroes' were already familiar. With red eyes, they were witch-doctors, almost sorcerers (especially those from the Diamant . . .[1]) — and therefore disturbing; there were also blue-eyed negroes, war-like colossi, whose origins were apparently in the West Cameroons. But it was these cat-eyed newcomers with long tapering hands and elegant pointed fingers that most troubled the imaginations of slaves and masters; very few knew such a breed existed, and to see two so alike seemed almost monstrous. It was hard to feel at ease in their presence.

---

[1] This region owes its name to a large diamond-shaped rock, about a mile from the coast and overlooking the wide bay.

They kept together all the time, and spoke to no one. When questioned, they frequently lifted their hands to their mouths and faces, as if reflecting, and one of them (it always seemed to be the same one) replied to the question after a moment, while the other moved his lips, faintly echoing the point. Separated, however briefly, they became considerably distressed.

When the sugar exploitation was progressing well, the black twins went to remind the honourable governor of his promise to free them.

'Those negroes,' said Lord Houël, 'are all the same with their vain dreams of freedom!'

And he clapped them in irons.

The twins, beating their breasts with their palms, cried out: 'O'O! . . .'

It was like a great belch from the stomach, deep and prolonged, a kind of grumbling which rose from the guts, rolled in the throat, and exploded in a shock-wave charged with hatred.

So it was that they were recognized as the descendants of O'O the Corsair or of O'Makendal. At that time, no one lived in such isolation as not to know of this episode. The trade winds gossip!

The rainy season was not yet over when a cyclone swept across the island. The slaves took advantage of it to start a terrible revolt; they ran, killing and plundering, in a gathering swarm. There were so many of them it was as though their fetters had broken of their own accord.

This was serious indeed. Negroes began to kill just as Christians would have done. A band led by a man nicknamed Jean-le-Blanc (John White, as black as treacle!) practised a scorched-earth policy from Basse-Terre to Capesterre, advancing with another band led by a certain Pèdre to join up with the two O'O (who had escaped and were plunging through the great forests of Sainte-Anne) at Pointe-à-Pitre, generally considered to be the social and commercial capital of the island. The angry negroes swore they would wreak vengeance on the killers of their fathers and children, would burn the town and the Béké[1] refugees, and would be utterly merciless if they met with the slightest resistance. This massed force, sowing terror as it went, was defeated by the weakness of

[1] Creole word for native whites.

Pèdre, who was taken in by Houël's promises. With Pèdre immobilized, Jean-le-Blanc was taken prisoner.

His task accomplished, Houël addressed a pallid Pèdre:

'Now, let's talk a bit about this liberty.'

The two ring-leaders, Pèdre and Jean-le-Blanc, racked, drawn and quartered with a few accomplices, were schooled in a suffering that only death could end. So much for that.

The O'O twins escaped, having learned from experience that a Béké never keeps his word, and tends to draw up a contract that is obviously disadvantageous to himself only if he has some ulterior motive.

Proud and obstinate, Houël gave the order, and the hunt for the twins began.

With Houël's pack at their heels, the twins were never in one place for long. If they found the circle closing in around them and there were fewer victims to vent their fury on, it is still true to say that it incited the slaves; they understood its determined nature and became passionately involved in the revolt, placing obstacles, even their very bodies, in the hunters' way.

To avoid traps, the twins separated. It was thought they would never leave each other, possessing two bodies certainly, but for all the world it seemed only one spirit, and one soul, governed by an intense instinctive life, a synchronized movement in defence and attack, as in retreat or in flight, dependent on disconcerting twinned manoeuvres, each in turn ceding the initiative to the other. So no one imagined they would ever split up. This last stratagem threw the hunters right off their trail. It was at once their twinship and their polarity that saved them. Much later it was discovered that one of them, hiding in the forests of Matouba, had joined forces with the last of the indestructible Caribbean Indians and so came into contact with the original Guadeloupe, that dark and mountainous ellipse from south to north where the clear contours of lovely valleys radiate outwards. As for the other, he worked with runaway slaves beyond the Rivière Sacré on the flat triangular island called Grand Terre. They say that he 'glanced from time to time towards the sea'.

Several revolts — in the Saintes, at Marie-Galante and Saint-Bartélemy — were ruthlessly put down. The tortures, as cowardly as their inventors, could have been more extreme; the negroes didn't flinch. Business in the America Island Company was so bad that it was dissolved, and Guadeloupe and its dependencies were sold to the Marquis de Roisseret. Colbert bought the island and ceded it to the West India Company which, on the brink of bankruptcy following numerous black revolts, had to return it to the king of France.

As slaves, the negroes hardly worried over the prosperity of their masters. It requires too great a virtue, to wear oneself out in sustaining someone else's fortune. The inspired O'O twins made trouble and started revolts at each worsening of the weather. God himself seemed to sanction their violence; each earthquake, cyclone and tidal wave was taken as a divine portent which drew out the long and terrible duel awaited feverishly by the negroes, who were both disturbed and submissive to its call. They had nothing more to lose. To die for their freedom: that was it. Of course, it was nothing more than a word; but also an idea that it was tempting to develop, and part of a deep kinship which stopped nevertheless at the colour of the skin. The White man struck, Christ in his fist. The Negro replied with the thunder of God. And alike as these two calamities were in their horror, the avenging act took on sacred significance.

It was Father Labat who solved the mystery of the 'seaward glance' and calmed things down somewhat. During one of his innumerable Caribbean voyages he captured, quite by chance, a tall negro with an appalling temper who sabotaged boats in the Bay of Moule. Even unarmed the 'savage' punched his assailants, sending them flying in a rapid burst: 'Bingue, Dingue, and Dingue!' Finally, he was overpowered by sheer force of numbers.

He was in such a state that no one realized quite who he was, especially as the man of God, against the promptings of his heart, alas! had him flogged and pickled.

Bent over a plank, 'Baindindingue' received fifty weighed and measured strokes of the cow-gut, allowing nothing but a double, untranslatable sound to escape his thick lips.

Each stroke lashed his shoulder-blades and a raw burning spread through his body. It came down over and over again. The varying angle of the cow-gut sounded a note that altered as it hit the upper or lower back, the shoulders, moved towards the neck or down towards the loins, biting into the buttocks until there was nothing but fire roaring in his ears to the beating of a drum. Though bound, the wretched body writhed and twisted, tensed and quivered. And while at its centre the red-hot pain flowed out and found relief only in a burn made more intense by its promise of final deliverance, a different, soothing heat fanned out into a miraculous rainbow.

Then, to avoid gangrene, a concoction of oils, spices, lemon and salt was applied to the raw flesh: 'There is nothing simpler nor more efficacious for assuaging tormented souls,' wrote the Dominican.

When the priest bent over the inert figure to check for any sign of life, he heard a groaning — two terrible syllables — and realized, dear God! that he held one of the O'O.

The circumspect Father Labat kept his lucky find to himself and looked after him. Then he shrewdly offered him his freedom in exchange for his knowledge of sugar-processing, arguing that the Church knew how to keep its promises. Since it was true that when priests made a pact — even with the devil — no one dared oppose it, Baindindingue accepted. But shrewder even than the Dominican, he demanded as guarantee — a white bride. Never at a loss for an answer, the Dominican agreed and handed over a redhead to the negro, a wretched girl picked up from a brothel on the coast of Brittany, and hustled on to a ship; her task was to 'populate' the American Islands. Abandoning her soul in utter misery, she was only too happy to be taken under the wing of the priests, even at the exorbitant price of having a savage in her bed.

A memorable document, transcribed by Father Labat himself into the endless accounts of his travels, states that O'O insisted that his liberty should be formalized before two witnesses, one white — the choice of Father Labat — and one black, chosen by Baindindingue, each of these witnesses being the father of at least four male children. At last, in the shade of a flame-tree, these undertakings were signed and sealed by mingling the blood of man and wife according to the African rite, and sprinkling it on the roots of the tree.

This decorative tree of Brazilian origin has serrated leaves in a pinnate structure, separate leaves arranged in parallel either side of the stem, like the sorb-tree. The flower has a red, regular corolla and separate petals, not unlike a wallflower. To the general stupefaction of reliable witnesses, this particular tree began to stir, then shudder, soughing like shaken brushwood as if governed by an intense, instinctive life. The purple corollas became irregular, with joined petals, like those of the tobacco plant, and turned a beautiful shade of blue.[1] Their surprise was even greater when, the same instant, that squat, thick-set tree, shut in by its weeping branches, raised itself, grew and opened towards the sky as if it had freed itself from some abhorrent and secular constraint. Some of the more susceptible observers took to their heels: it's hard to keep calm when a fallen giant rises to his feet. Father Labat proclaimed it a miracle. Surely no one could doubt his powers of foresight now. The races could mix! And nature rejoiced in it. In all the transport of revelation, the Dominican could do no other than keep his promise.

O'O Baindindingue was the first black slave in the Antilles to win his freedom after a long struggle. This amazing event was called 'The Miracle of the Flame-Tree'.

And indeed, who would ever have thought that a tree could turn from red to blue and a negro become free?

To fulfil his side of the strange contract made with Father Labat, O'O undertook to instruct two whites and two blacks in the art of extracting cane-juice, of clarifying it before it concentrated and crystallized, then of separating it to extract Kio sugar, and finally showing them the natural way (supernatural ones being barred) of whitening the Kio sugar and of using the remaining molasses to concoct 'tafia' rum.

Houël was surprised when a little later he realized that the priests were in competition with him, and were setting up refineries of industrial proportions not only all over Guadeloupe but in Martinique as well. And what is more, they were marketing tafia, that well-known beverage which, sad to say, exerts a sway over souls that has been amply demonstrated . . .

At the time when Father Labat was reaping a vast fortune from the sale of white sugar and rough tafia produced thanks to O'O

[1] Around the Great Lakes in Africa numerous blue flame-trees alternate with red ones, especially on the shores of Lake Tanganyika. The red flowers are of the non-hermaphroditic, diclinous type, with pistils constituting the female organ; the blue are also diclinous, but with stamens containing grains of pollen, the famous male substance.

Baindindingue's secrets, Guadeloupe and her dependencies consisted of three main parishes or communes, with about twenty churches and a hundred sugar-works and refineries. The population of around twelve thousand was made up two-thirds of negroes and mulattos and one-third of whites. A mere twenty original Caribbean Indians remained. . . . The freed blacks living in the communes began to enter commerce and industry, or became workers, while some owned land which they cultivated.

Having scrupulously fulfilled his contract, O'O Baindaindingue built his own refinery at Saint-François and purchased some cane-fields at Sainte-Anne. Through whim or reason, or perhaps through love, his wife the 'redhead' embraced the slaves and their cause more ardently than the priests might have wished, concealing them in the attic of the curacy or behind the chapel altar when they escaped from plantations. Then she escorted them in person towards the great forests of Sainte-Anne or to the Soufrière, the home of O'O Souf, where there was no chance of their being found.

The situation was precarious. Louis XIV's different decrees rained down upon the colony. Guadeloupe had to come to heel under the general governance of Martinique, which had made its fortune since the inhabitants, in their turn, had learnt from Father Labat how to whiten sugar. Moreover, the Sun King granted the first legal recognition to the 'Trade', thereby regularizing a commercial racket which until then had been carried on in secret. With the application of the Edict of Nantes came the Black Code of Colbert! After the war against the English, during which the blacks, led by Father Labat, as always covered themselves with glory, Louis XIV took steps to raise a barrier between the black and white populations, stopping, for example, the mixed unions which had been made fashionable by the rash Dominican. Finally, a decree declared that all liberty unsanctioned by the administrative authority was null and void. Houël, or his successors, demanded vengeance. O'O with his redhead from Sainte-Anne only just had time to get clear and join O'O Souf on the well-fortified Soufrière, leaving their two children at the chaplaincy. They were twins.

It was not without perverse intent that the fugitives left behind their offspring, of mixed blood, but oddly enough, black as ebony and ferocious with it. Several strange stories circulated about what tradition calls the 'Big Twins'. Within the confines of the parish, where they received a religious education, with its humanist tradition and attendant dogmas and disciplines, the little negroes were as gentle as could be; but the merest kick from the superintendent, some slight offhandedness or the tiniest hint of an aspersion triggered off a complex psychic reaction: the cherubs turned white, red or yellow before one's eyes.

The crossing of a black with a redhead, in a troubled age, seems to have produced a highly explosive mixture, not unlike nitroglycerine. Some kind of trigger is necessary and, if these conditions are satisfied, nothing can stop the release of destructive potential. Compress the viscous liquid into a container, or confine the little boys to close quarters; prepare a small detonator and prime the explosive with mercuric fulminate, or say something disagreeable even in jest to the little monsters, and you will see how a reign of terror begins.

All external stimulus of a certain kind had deep physical repercussions and caused instant disturbance: plantation fires, pillage, rape, slave revolts. And so it was that at the age of fourteen they ran away from the curacy because one had had his ear slightly tweaked, but really very lightly, while the other was not touched at all. That very night a chapel was in flames! Recaptured, the twins were racked, lashed and seasoned with spice in the proper manner. Far from wanting them dead, the priests wished to lead them back to the straight and narrow path. With their primitive instincts, flat noses, big greedy lips and the wiry hair characteristic of all of them, the negroes were animals adopted through a Christian generosity which was keen to root out the evil in them.

The twins were incurable, so to speak. Inveterate runaways, several times punished and pardoned, Father Labat had shown such generosity, but here they were again, the ungrateful little fiends, rebelling without a cause.

When a negro like O'O Baindaindingue takes flight and leaves his children behind like hostages, he is perfectly aware of what he is doing.

Vast land clearings were underway in the colony in preparation for new cultivation, such as coffee, to compensate for the financial disaster following the Sun King's famous Law. Ruined landowners from the metropolis came personally to direct their island developments; of course the heavy work fell to the slaves. Born for misfortune and suffering, once again pressurized, harassed and discouraged, in the fear and prostration of the present, and full of anxiety over the tragic days ahead, all, all waited for the chance to revolt. It came quickly.

The sight of two little black boys running for their lives across fields, pursued by mastiffs and keepers armed with long whips, over-excited the workers. Those children were going to be torn to shreds by the contemptible dogs. They must have been maltreated or insulted and had hit back. Now they were going to be killed and flayed alive and given as meat to the mastiffs. How could they be saved?

Fever rose. Fear invaded hearts and minds. Fear, shame, revolt. If one considers actions, and what can provoke the overflow of rage, then reason can help our understanding. The little black boys ran like mongooses, rolling their small buttocks. Stark naked and quivering like arrows, jaws gaping in the flash of a backward glance, they urged each other on, the one sprinting ahead of the other in a supreme effort that emptied him of breath, then, dropping behind, he paced himself with the long, rapid strides that went before him and kept him going. In this relay system, with their teeth clenched and their eyes fixed on the hillocks and thickets, going all out for the great forests, their faces, their bodies, their whole being, their souls, their little negro souls strained towards the supreme hope of freedom.

Their small bare feet hit the earth:

— Flap! flap! flap!

And the hills in feeble echo went:

— Flop! . . . flop! . . . flôô!

sounding against the growlings of dogs and the whistle of whiplashes cutting the air. The plantation negroes started to cry out, quietly at first, then louder and louder:

'O'O! . . . O'O!'

and in faster and faster rhythm:

'O'O! . . . O'O!'

'O'O! . . . O'O! . . . O'O!'

'O'O! . . . O'O! . . . O'O! . . . O'O!'

The boys took courage and made up ground.

— Flap . . . flap . . .

— Flap . . . flap . . . flap . . .

— Flap . . . flap . . . fô . . . ô . . .

From all the surrounding fields, these strange onomatopoeic sounds punctuated the pursuit:

'O'O! . . . O'O!'

'O'O! . . . O'O! . . . O!'

'O'O! . . . O'O! . . . O! . . . O!'

The huts emptied. Everyone started running behind the keepers. The keepers followed the mastiffs and urged them on; the dogs tailed the children; the children tensed their muscles:

— Flap! flap – flap . . .

— Flap! flap – flap! . . .

The rabble followed; each man gripped a cutlass.

'O'O! . . . O'O!'

'O'O! . . . O'O! . . . O!'

The tom-tom beat out the rhythm:

—Bangue!

— Bidip — Bandambangue!

— Ababa, ababa!

Everyone ran in one great free-for-all.

'O'O! . . . O'O!'

— Bandangue!

— Taca, tacata . . .

— Ababa! . . . ababa!

— Bangue! . . . O'O! . . . Bip! . . . Bidip!

— Frii! . . . Flap!

— Fô . . . O! . . . O!

Bamboos and sticks; stretched skins, vibrating to rhythm and cadence; songs and sounds; sounds and cries in the clearness:

'O! O!'

— Bangue.

— Bidip, Bip!

'O'!'

— Flap! . . . Flii . . .

Flight within flight, rhythm within rhythm; movement and cadence in the drunken progress towards death:

'Halt!'

'Never!'

'O! O!'

— Flap — flap . . . Oww!!

Cries. Chants. Dances. Brawls. It was appalling — dogs slaughtered, keepers cut to mincemeat; houses and chapels on fire; rapes, screams and death, everywhere death, one extraordinary surge of death. Such is violence. Who wanted it? . . . And killing. Ababa! . . . Ababa!

Troops had to be called out to stem the tide of this great uprising. After one massacre came another, which was put down by yet another. Flames, the stake, group drownings, mass executions, the more refined tortures — anything so long as there was blood and screaming. Violence! And the blood of violence! Ababa! . . . Ababa!

Later, the twins figured among a list of names, all known to history, Le Sueur, Moutier, Liégard, Bologne, Audet, Barin, Ducastrou, Congras, Bridou, Lépine, Bocquet, Dorton and Clatière. Latulipe and some of his companions were taken. They were racked and then hanged. Punishments were meted out to a great many negroes; whether they were innocent or guilty scarcely mattered, they had to be held up as examples.

A price was put on the twins' heads.

In fact, capturing them would have changed nothing; but as no one managed to do so it was much the worse, since the knowledge that they were still at large kept alive the terror.

At this time, Guadeloupe had nearly 50,000 inhabitants, of whom 45,000 were slaves, each dreaming of becoming O'O.

The number of slaves increased with the chances of quick profit. The Black Code hardened accordingly, to keep the negroes in the servitude they would not accept. Any slave who took to the hills was to be brought down, and killed if he tried again. Blacks were forbidden to marry Whites, and any Béké who wished to take a negress for a spouse was liable to a heavy fine. Before he died, Louis XIV laid the foundations of the most abhorrent legislation in human history. The Sun King! . . . But faces burned by the sun would not accept him as ruler, and revolt followed revolt. The wholesome array of corporal punishments efficiently put everyone in the proper place assigned him by the Almighty. God made man in his image. God is therefore white, for only the white man can be in the image of God; it follows that the negro, who cannot be in the image of God, cannot be a man either. QED. . . The chains of society were forged by such hammers of theory and tautological example. But while this Holy Law, said to come from God, was being preached in churches, two black giants — devils to be sure — appeared and disappeared leaving a trail of blood along their path. Punishments and tortures were diversified, such as severing the hamstrings of those who tried to escape. But the revolts persisted, and when some were overcome by despair, they would slit their children's throats to deliver them from slavery, and then fling themselves in front of a galloping horse, ensuring the rider's death as well as their own. Runaway slaves hid in the heights of the Soufrière, and in the woods of Pointe-Noire and Sainte-Rose. Whole families took refuge in these forests, living in the most primitive conditions, but free.

Then, in 1780, the most appalling cyclone ever recorded struck the islands. Guadeloupe, Martinique, Jamaica, St Lucia, St Vincent and Dominica were devastated. In the tidal wave the sea rose eight metres, sweeping away innumerable dwellings. The cathedral at Fort-de-France was carried away, and at Saint-Vincent reefs of coral were torn from the seabed and flung up on to the shore. No one dared to estimate the number of victims, mostly slaves, who were carried off by the tempest; and those that did escape developed an even greater aptitude for suffering: they were put back to work under the whip. The fewer they were, the more they had to rebuild, replant and harvest. It is really impossible to take in the number of crimes committed. The negro knew he was wretched, because he was; but he became great because he knew it, and had the strength to rise against his oppressor despite the multiple punishments.

Louis XIV bequeathed the Black Code. Louis XV invented or reinvented the stake: in pyramid formation, negroes were flung wholesale into the flames. Louis XVI carried on the tradition. But the slaves persisted in their demand for freedom. And at that time in history many men, both black and white, were struggling for it. The idea was in fashion.

On 4 January 1793 a small troop of negroes armed with cutlasses, spears and arrows was seen coming down from the Soufrière and from Matouba to Saint-Claude, and from Saint-Claude to Basse-Terre. At its head was a giant with glowing eyes, supple movements and a cat-like roll to his hips.

The news spread like wildfire through the country. The giant conches trumpeted from hill to hill, and the tom-tom spread it abroad from island to island:

'*O'O ka descendent.*' (The O'O are coming.)

'*Mi O'O, mi!*' (Here are the O'O, here they are!)

In fact, one of the Big Twins, with some followers, was coming to confront Viscount Arotte, temporary governor of Guadeloupe, with a demand that the Law of Emancipation passed by the new French Republic be implemented immediately.

But the Viscount had fled to a neighbouring colony; and General Collot, emissary of the new Republic, had not yet arrived.

Far out to sea, Captain Lacrosse's frigate, the *Félicité*, was cruising towards land, and instead of a flag, the revolutionary's red bonnet flew at the masthead.

Even before it arrived, the O'O knew that with it came Liberty.

But the guards at the governor's residence, left without instructions and panic-stricken at the appearance of one of the twins, felled him on the spot.

Thus it was that at ninety years of age (according to the curacy records) one of the Big Twins, son of O'O Baindindingue and the redhead, was slain.

When they received news of the murder, the negroes who held the town started one of the most terrifying massacres in the history of Guadeloupe. The frigate bringing Liberty dared not approach Basse-Terre and set sail for Pointe-à-Pitre, where Lacrosse came ashore the next day.

On the quay, the other twin waited with a young man by his side. Lacrosse ran up to the old man, and embraced him with the fraternal kiss of the Republic.

It was, of course, one of the Big Twins that Lacrosse embraced on the quay at Pointe-à-Pitre. The other, as we know, was murdered at Basse-Terre.

The two slaves captured by Houël at Saint-Martin eventually escaped; one of them, O'O Baindindingue, hid in the forests of Sainte-Anne, while O'O Souf took refuge on the Soufrière, or in the forests of Matouba, both swearing vengeance on a gross injustice:

the breaking of a word of honour. They were deeply convinced that no real or permanent justice could be attained without violent means; remarkable men, motivated by a continual thirst to strike a fair balance between rights and duties.

It is not known at what period they were joined by the Big Twins, the sons of O'O Baindindingue, who continued the fight. What obsessed the twins was the idea of Liberty, and this was connected in their minds with virility. They made their presence felt, had no use for compromise, and were rarely seen without a cutlass between their teeth.

In fact, the tradition that dubbed this pair the Big Twins could never tell them apart, so it is impossible to say which was killed at Basse-Terre and which died in Pointe-à-Pitre. Usually, one was never far behind the other, and no one knew for sure how to distinguish them, for they dressed the same: bare chests and leather corsair breeches, subtle white in colour — everyone said it was Béké skin — and close scrutiny of their faces revealed no distinguishing feature or even expression. One was killed as he demanded the Law, the other collapsed as he was given it, and after their deaths no one could remember if both had indeed existed, or if they weren't in fact one and the same person at the mercy of some capricious sprite. Tradition shut its eyes to all but one twin, henceforth immortal.

The boy standing beside the O'O greeted by Lacrosse was none other than the grandson of the Big Twins. He was called O'Baindingue (not to be confused with O'O Baindindingue, his grandfather).

His ancestor, O'O the Corsair, or if you prefer, O'O the Pirate, came originally from Timbuctoo. No matter where he came from, he will always be considered the first of the African heroes to fight against slavery. He himself had twins, by a little negress: O'O Baindindingue, who could deal three punches for one — 'Baingue! dingue! dingue! . . .' — and O'O Souf. This latter lived like a hermit in one of the caves of the Soufrière, the 'Grotte aux Amis', a huge overhanging rock that could shelter a dozen people. One can still visit the summit of this active volcano above Basse-Terre. O'O Souf spent his whole life in an infernal cavern and stank of sulphur — hence his name. He was taciturn and appeared rarely, always recognizable by his smell.

O'O Baindindingue married a redhead and thus brought about the miracle of the flame-tree. She gave birth to two sons, known as the Big Twins. One of the sons of the Big Twins was famous as a lifelong runaway, not once reduced to slavery. He lived in the forests and knew like no one else how to appear and disappear in a clap of thunder, leaving no trace, so no Béké ever spotted him. He operated like a pirate, watching his prey from a distance, springing upon it, and disappearing before he could be identified. These tactics brought the original old sea-dog to mind, and he was known quite simply as O'O.

The prefix O'O is the most honourable of names. Its twin syllables, full of sound, evoke the double purity of sky and sea, elements that mould the very soul of the slave. O'O was replaced by O', to identify descendants of these legendary heroes. So it was that the boy who witnessed Lacrosse embracing his grandfather came to bear the name O'Baindingue.

Alas! He too was to undergo all that his ancestors had. Free in 1793, when he must have been about ten years old, there he was in 1802, about nineteen and once more in slavery. He too had to become a runaway.

No sooner had the whites re-established the system which reduced the negroes to forced labour than they repented doing so. New sanctions fortified the slaves' determination.

As a runaway, O'Baindingue struggled desperately for that 'Liberty' which had troubled Houël so little. He too became an almost legendary figure, in that the undeniable historical facts in which he participated, corroborated by the chronicle of family and place-names that still exist in the Antilles, seem now to belong to some vague historical narrative rather than to a precisely charted epic.

One revolt scarcely amounted to much, and there was hardly any difference between the day of victory and what preceded it: all had to be begun again, but feelings ran high, courage returned, and bitterness increased.

Thus it was that O'Baindingue was an active participant in the heroic battle waged by Delgrès[1] against General Richepanse, who

---

[1] A mulatto from Martinique who struggled heroically against Richepanse in Guadeloupe. Defeated on 28 May 1802, Delgrès nevertheless set alight the powder which was to shake oppressed and oppressor alike.

had come in Bonaparte's name to re-establish slavery in Guadeloupe. The negro fought against Lacrosse himself, who had received 'Additional Instructions' from Bonaparte, and created the 'Forest Hunting Corps', a pitiless militia that trained dogs to tear negroes apart, and that tortured, hanged, drowned and shot according to the methods perfected by Carrier at Nantes. They even went so far as to set a slave astride a blade in an iron cage, leaving him there until he was sliced in two — a torture lasting a day or so.

As more negroes were killed, it became less common to hail them as martyrs for meeting their deaths in a great cause. Everyone was now convinced that they could only obtain what they had the strength to conquer.

They had no sense that they were playing a part in the history of the world, or even in the destiny of their time, a naïve aspiration of religious souls, always trying to flatter themselves and always hearing their own words as 'voices' emanating from beyond them. No, the negroes' fight had nothing to do with sublime exegesis, it was above all an impulse in the blood, an instinctive feeling that each should take account of his neighbour and understand him. The slaves would not leave hold until they could impose themselves on the universal conscience. The runaways apparently took to their heels, but in that flight they multiplied, and sought refuge in the forests, only to break out in greater numbers later. The day would come when they had to be reckoned with. Which it did, in the explosion of 1848.

Like his grandfather before him, O'Baindingue went to confront the authorities, in the form of Governor Layrle, with his demand for Liberty. History was caricaturing itself. And like his grandfather, he held one of his descendants by the hand, who was already well-known to his compatriots. This was O'Dingue 'the Mad', and everyone knew what that meant.

O'Dingue was tall, fine and distinguished, with green eyes like a cat's.

Governor Layrle welcomed O'Baindingue, but kept clear of O'Dingue. With a sword in his right hand and a cutlass in his left, he crossed arms right in front of the Governor when he drew near.

'That's O'Dingue,' someone said to him. 'Take care, sir!'

The Governor kept his distance, for the man obviously *was* mad.

As a matter of fact, when the news of Emancipation finally reached Guadeloupe, it had already, strange to say, been proclaimed . . .

There were no more troops, no more guards greeting with rifle shots men bearing white flags. There was nothing at all to fall back on, and the whites could be annihilated at the sound of a terrible signal:

'O'O! . . .'

It was too late now to bolt the doors.

Some say that O'Dingue arranged for this signal to be given simultaneously in several towns where, on the instant, ferocious bands of slaves appeared, cutlasses at the ready. They leapt over the cannon pointed at them, snatched the cannonballs, and gave themselves over to a hideous orgy of killing.

After a few warnings of this kind, Governor Layrle could do no other than proclaim Liberty, long before receiving the official message from Schoelcher. O'Dingue intended to make quite clear this Liberty had not merely been conceded, but conquered, and that he was prepared to commit any madness to safeguard it.

Do not believe he wasn't capable of worse. We shall see.

ALONG a clear, shallow and generally calm sea, bounded by its coral reef, stretches the beach of Sainte-Anne.

Not far off rises Vallet bluff, a high-point in a painful epoch.

A white house made of bevelled stone and roofed with red tiles stands out against its curves — a veritable rock at the crest of a green and scented grove. The centuries have left it almost intact, a witness to the great social changes taking place on the Islands. The walls are nothing less than ramparts, and the doors and windows, well-fitted as they are, still give the impression of apertures in the sides of a fortress. The interior is admirably ventilated. The ground floor is used as a dining-cum-sitting room, and opens on to a veranda facing the sea, with smoking-rooms in the wings. The first floor contains several rooms embellished with balconies in the Spanish style, and at the top of the house is an attic with sloping roofs, fitted with skylights that let the sun into the darkest corners.

The Békés built it. The O'O requisitioned it, and O'Dingue, the grandson of O'O, furbished it to his taste. The large living-room was now laid with oriental carpets, and furnished with comfortable mahogany furniture in the American colonial style — very rare pieces in the Antilles. There were bamboo chairs and rockers, and, on the wall, large frescoes of seascapes: slavers being chased by corsairs, and Trafalgar-style boardings, or tragic episodes in the life of the slave, like that famous 'auction' which shows a negress on her knees, begging her purchaser to buy her child who is also up for sale, while the well-born white gentleman snickers at the 'savage's' useless tears. Line and colour harmonize in images at once mawkish, strange and poignant. The servant girls, circulating endlessly among them, humming old and melancholy tunes as they go, seem to have stepped straight out of such a canvas.

Large cultivated patches spread down the flanks of the bluff. Towards the sea, coconut-trees shake dishevelled heads in the wind, while here and there are lines and groves of palm-trees. Inland, sugar-cane plantations raise golden plumes, and right alongside stand the 'Factory' and its 'Forge'. Much further off lies the dark forest of the Grands-Fonds, an impenetrable jungle haunted by tragic memories.

Right here, flocks of duck and bunting pick about, while over there skittish foals stretch and prance, and little groups of cows, observed by the dark, imposing silhouettes of bulls, chew the cud. Each has his own patch on this prodigiously fertile land. Do not stray within the limits each species has marked out more instinctively and more certainly than any man-made fence could do: the bird takes flight with warning cries, the colt stamps his hoof, and the horned beast bears down on the intruder like a thunderbolt. Like their human fellows, animals take on hereditary traits, vices and perhaps curses, which drive them to stake out territories, invisible but deadly!

Vallet was long considered as a bandits' staging-post, not to be traversed except by invitation. It is said of O'Dingue, the last of the runaway slaves, that he would have leapt at the chance to hasten emancipation, let loose terror, and take advantage of the ensuing public disorder to fill his coffers.

He 'purchased' Vallet, and moved in. Where once he had been a slave, he was now master, and his numerous servants cowered before his gaze. Those who weren't prepared to put in the hard and varied work indispensable to a vast agricultural development backed up by a sugar refinery, a distillery and a large forge; those who didn't knuckle down to the daily routine of running a great house, were beaten or condemned to die of hunger along with their wives and children. The conquest of freedom was a trial for everyone, but workers' rights remained a long way off for many. They hadn't yet learned how to organize themselves and so remained defenceless. Some stood up for themselves: they could offer their services elsewhere and give away production secrets, supposing any remained in the sugar and rum industries. Above all, for those in other parts who had avoided the authority of an O'O, a new weapon lay to hand, as yet untried: the strike. But O'Dingue, married to a Hindu Indian (which was typical of his family's search for multiracial unions, even though their skin remained black), employed more and more Malabars — Indians from the East rather than the West — who could be moulded at will and put to work. He was no dreamer. He began to give orders like a Béké. Those who through ill-luck depended on him, looked back nostalgically to the good old days of slavery.

He was not unique. All the great landowners, black and white, lengthened the working day, lowered wages, and appointed the weakest men — in particular the vulnerable foreign workers — to the most desirable positions. In the name of 'Liberty' a potentially seductive order was established, but it was soon revealed as the product of universal human selfishness. All revolutionary effort meets with good and evil, and gives birth to their offspring.

Nothing in O'Dingue disposed him to compassion. He wanted mastery. Having trembled for his life for so long, he in his turn perpetuated cruelties. From what they could see, the Békés blushed to find in him an image of themselves, while the negroes ran away as fast as they could. He was a hard man, an authoritarian, who ruled over his factories and his large property (some two hundred and fifty acres) and even that of his neighbours. He lorded it over the town, the neighbouring communes, and over nearly all the lovely stretch of country from Gosier to Sainte-Anne, right up to Moule, where he and his family had compelled the Matignon-Whites[1] to live in a state of poverty worse than that of the black peasants around them. Nothing whatever escaped his authority, directly or indirectly, with the exception of a few isolated pockets still controlled by whites who had been reduced to acting with the utmost caution.

He took personal control of the sugar-mill and distillery, leaving the forge to one of his brothers, and the cane-fields in the care of one of his mulatto half-brothers: real negroes weren't born to work the earth! . . . If ever he spotted a worker not taking due care in polishing a still, he would swoop down and break his arm. The factory had to be cleaned daily, like a ship, and as regular as clockwork! Latecomers were sacked . . . It was tough work. However good or bad the year, a thousand tons of sugar and two hundred barrels of rum had to be produced.

Agricultural production, under the management of Tonton-Hubé (a mulatto who was supposedly a bastard of the O'O clan), was also kept working at white-hot speed to feed the factory.

---

[1] A few whites lived on in the Moule forests, descendants of the Matignon who refused to free his slaves in accordance with the decree of 1848. A legend connects these 'Old-Whites', who lived in rigorous seclusion, with the ancestors of the Prince of Monaco.

Tonton-Hubert wasn't always a pleasure to meet either, though quite different from his black half-brother. At that time, every mulatto dreamt of being black, or even better, white. He affected no such aspirations. He was as tough on himself as he was on others, always hard at it in the struggle against poverty. He was in his thirties, well-built, with a domed forehead that was harder than macadam; he had red eyes (rather than green or blue) which related him more to the witch-doctors from the Diamant in Martinique, than to a Baindingue. During the Emancipation troubles, his father raped a white woman and left her for dead. But not long after, this union produced a most peculiar fruit, abandoned by its mother at birth. Getting wind of this child with coffee-coloured skin, the negro brought him home, recognized him and presented him as a twin for O'Dingue, the eldest of his legitimate sons. Only an O'O could decide that black and mulatto brothers, with a ten-year interval between them, could be twins . . . And did such a thing make people snicker? If one valued one's life, it was dangerous so much as to smile furtively at this eccentricity. Hubert, as he was called, was born on 3 November, feast of the patron saint of hunters, and soon became the favourite, for whom his father would have done anything. He grew up with O'Dingue, closer than his shadow, and though it would not have been impossible for him to share his thirst for mastery, he preferred to take second place as a matter of choice and tactics, inspiring fear and respect wherever he went because of the mystery in his eyes.

There were over a thousand plantation workers — four hundred of whom were Indians — under the iron rod of this singular mulatto. They took care of the manuring, tilling and preparation of the cane plantations. Harvest-time was hardest of all because conditions were difficult, and quick, efficient work was crucial. It was often carried out under a looming cyclone. Tonton-Hubé had his own peculiar way of judging people. He could root out sluggards and track down thieves. Then he would take them somewhere private and, as a warning, would tear one of their teeth out with a pair of tongs . . . He was everywhere. Each and every person expected him to swoop down upon them at any moment. Was he cruel? And if he was, could he not also show kindness from time to time? . . . When, thanks to his mysterious sixth sense he discovered neither a thief nor a scrounger, and still less a good-for-nothing he could sack there and then, but a soul in distress, he would stop at nothing — even cruelty — to save him and keep him on. Old, violent ways persisted, and if, despite universal suffrage, privileged blacks and mulattos occasionally behaved towards the mass of the population as once the whites had done, this upright, imposing man earned respect rather than loathing, for he was fair and free from hatred.

In fact, he was a red-eyed mulatto, and a better witch-doctor than the renowned red negroes. No one believes in such remedies any more, but he could bring speedy relief to a serious wound from an axe or scythe by filling the wound with fine salt. Of course it stung horribly. To staunch a haemorrhage he would sprinkle the wound with fine ground coffee. Even today, his treatment of renal colic is astonishing. It is quite harmless, and can be tried in western latitudes and longitudes: a spoonful of honey and, as a preventative, a regular dose of it, neat or with milk. . . . To all who worked under him, he recommended a certain plant for the treatment of dysentery, a prevalent complaint of the time. This plant is known as 'bismuth' in Martinique, 'crab's herb' in Guadeloupe, and 'Seymour's herb' in Capesterre, after the major who imported it from Cuba. In Sainte-Anne, the same miracle plant rejoices in the strange names of 'broken knee' or 'pulled knee'. Stems and leaves are boiled, and three cups of this tisane, taken on three consecutive days, will cure diarrhoea or dysentery. For migraine, inhale the extract of lemon. For gonorrhea, he recommended boiling twenty leaves of 'Cassia-alata' in a litre of water, adding three teaspoonfuls of lemon juice. One glass to be drunk morning and evening, and another to be taken by enema. Three litres of this medicine would cure the imprudent soul if diagnosed in time. But it was advisable to consult a doctor, rather than ask him to cure syphilis, for he would explain that the easiest way to avoid contracting it was not to expose oneself to it. Only fools laugh at chastity, he would say, and continence never did anyone any harm. He claimed that the early marriage of healthy citizens who had kept their virginity for the procreation of sturdy children, combined with marital fidelity, were the two best protections against venereal disease. He himself took no mistresses: who can tell the sort of stuff a red mulatto's made of?

When the needy went to him for advice, he worked more by instinct than reason.

The other brothers of O'Dingue looked after the business at Pointe-à-Pitre and Basse-Terre, where they dealt with the transport of goods by ox-cart, though one of them ran an island-to-island trading business with a schooner, selling off rum here, sugar there, and bringing home tobacco from Cuba, cod from Terre-Neuve, and cattle from Trinidad. Thick as thieves, they were extremely active, and always attentive to the instructions, or rather orders, issued by their big brother O'Dingue. Though somewhat jealous of Hubert's exceptional position, they were nevertheless relieved not to have the immense responsibility of running the plantation, a task which required a great deal of knowledge both of people and practicalities.

They were always busy in the fields, in the forge — the blacksmith was a redoubtable O'O, the kindly clodhopper of the clan — or engaged in transporting and marketing their products. Still others watched over the Béké's dealings, and chased his daughters. There was always some duel to be fought, and they dreamed of nothing but civil strife and heroic confrontations. There were not only men to be beaten down, but fixed ideas and prejudice as well. The intolerable behaviour of the whites towards the blacks continued despite Emancipation, and they attacked them for it at every possible opportunity. They excelled above all in sword-play, and were rarely wounded when they took the trouble of consulting the celebrated 'Tonton'. Only O'Dingue, the uncontested master, had no need of Tonton-Hubé's tips to liquidate whoever it might be with efficiency and despatch. His long and flexible rapier could dent the finest blade, while his deadly aim with the pistol sent the bullet clean through his opponent's right eye. He was always spoiling for a fight with the Békés, to oust them from the Island's administration, and with wide gestures of his arms and slender hands would offer his opinion that the black race of the Antilles would be emancipated without Schoelcher, or in spite of Schoelcher, and that in consequence no white traces would remain in the country.

When he spoke like this the negroes egged him on with flattery, exclaiming with their mouths wide open:

'Oh! . . . O'Dingue . . .'

and even:

'O'O Dingue!'

so that when people saw him pass in the town a rumour started up:

'Look, O'O, look!'

as if transported back to the old days.

Count de Lériv, a rich Breton aristocrat whose ancestor the Red Corsair came to the American islands with a sharp sword, a Stradivarius violin[1] and golden cutlery, which enabled him to earn his bread and butter as the expression goes — *he* never said on seeing the negro go past:

'Here comes O'Dingue!'

instead he would exclaim:

'There goes 'Le Dingue', the Madman!'

He thought to himself: 'There's the man to be brought down, bound and shut in a cage'. He saw him already straddling a sabre. He was a menace to whites and blacks alike, a veritable public calamity.

If you leave the church of Sainte-Anne on your right and follow the road towards Pointe-à Pitre, you come to Durivage, a vast property stretching the whole length of a beach. From this Mansion Count de Lériv observed the comings and goings of O'Dingue on Vallet bluff, resolving to do away with him at the first possible opportunity. The sly Breton bided his time. And the O'O, craftier still, likewise lay in wait for him.

---

[1] The violin bore the inscription: *Antoninus Stradivarius Cremonenfis. Faciebat Anno 1721.*

AFTER the anarchist revolt, aggravated by the savagery which accompanies all social revolutions, Guadeloupe was plunged into an economic depression. Since the agricultural labourers were now free, they lost all desire to work and spent their time drifting about, so that the country's sole source of income was jeopardized. Out-of-work negroes wandered from bar to bar, quarrelled amongst themselves, and generally had it in for everyone. Having finally conquered something, they were apparently dissatisfied because the result was not quite what they had expected. But they were always ready to fight for their ideal, if only someone could tell them what that ideal really was. The profoundly altered relationship between blacks and whites created a serious problem. A letter to the Governor of Pointe-à-Pitre from a certain Corot, dated 26 October 1848, notes that:

> The negroes refuse to do anything. The opportunity always open to them for selling herbs, coal, wood and sugar cane to the nearby town, is the principal cause of their refusal to work. What is more, the priest has told them that Friday shall be washing-day, Saturday being reserved for selling their produce and Sunday consecrated exclusively to God. Marriages are to take place on Tuesdays and it is only right that everyone should attend . . . On Thursdays mass is said for certain needy souls and is not to be missed . . . So you see what is left, honourable Governor! We know how difficult it is to re-establish some semblance of order, especially today when the task is that much harder than it was in terms of principle, made so by the relaxation and lack of energy we have all suffered from so much. But you will surely, in your wisdom, take some preliminary measures to prepare the way for the severer ones we so badly need.[1]

On top of this explosive state of affairs, a new breed of

[1] Victor Schoelcher, *Correspondance inédite*, II, *Lettres martiniquaises (1829–1881)*, with a preface by Jean-Louis Jeune (*Revue Mondiale*, Paris, 1935).

opportunists arrived in the country and stayed just long enough to exploit the situation. They spread rumours about anything and everything, inciting people to all kinds of action, including setting fire to the town of Pointe-à-Pitre in August 1871. Then they cleared out, having sown the seeds of slander, left debts unpaid, or murdered to escape them. But sometimes they fell victim to their own temerity in a country whose people were used to looking death in the face.

The general terror was such that no one dared undertake anything. To reverse completely the popular state of mind and to shepherd men into regular, ordered and disciplined employment, was to swim hopelessly against the current of the time. Only whites and blacks able to organize themselves and reimpose old-style forced labour profited from this state of affairs and, paradoxically, worked for the benefit of the country at the same time. But they did so under very difficult conditions, always vulnerable to the least incident, suspecting each other of the lowest motives, and ready to destroy each other on quite futile pretexts.

O'Dingue and de Lériv, thoroughbred bosses, were at daggers drawn, even though, had they co-operated, they would have consolidated their fortune and that of Guadeloupe. Peace between blacks and whites — neither of whom could exercise the aboriginals' historic rights — seemed to be the way forward.

An unforeseen event ignited the whole thing.

As a child, Count de Lériv's daughter had been sent to the convent at Versailles, a famous school for the daughters of the nobility in the Basse-Terre area, not far from the Champ d'Arbaud. Then, following the custom among rich families, she was sent to Paris where she acquired a higher level of learning than the nuns offered, and a taste for free-thinking.

Above all she benefited from a musical education, for she had inherited the Red Corsair's talent: he is said to have entertained his crew, between two boardings, by playing the violin. With her pretty face and blond mane, tall, slim, well-developed figure, one could divine the woman in the girl from the moment she arrived home, at eighteen years of age.

She soon made her début in Creole society. Life opened its doors to her. All the neighbouring nobility was invited to the

'Homecoming Ball' organized to celebrate her return. Such great parties were a time-honoured practice among families who wanted to know each other better, and for young men and women to plan their futures, while the old could look on and reminisce. In a heady atmosphere of 'schruub' — rum in which orange peel had been soaked for years — 'chaudô' — vanilla cream steeped in rum — and bumper glasses of fresh or sweetened coconut milk, naturally scented with rum, backed up by 'accras' and 'chiquetaille' — cod frittered or shredded and snacks sprinkled with pepper — couples gracefully closed and separated, joyfully smiling and gazing one another fondly in the eye. They waltzed or danced polkas, mazurkas and Scottish reels in the reception hall where the orchestra was installed, under the veranda, and even in the garden between small tables covered with spotless white cloths, gold-edged china, and shining glasses continually filled with punch by eager serving-girls. Red petals from the flame-tree were strewn over the ground. Garlands of different flowers hung from the roof and brightened the corners of each room.

The Count knew how to spend his gold on lamps that would show the lights in the eyes of those young women full of gaiety, hungry for dancing and pleasure. Each had had her 'Homecoming Ball'. Some had found their desired companion, others were busy doing so, others would have to wait some time yet for that great moment, if not for ever. The Count was a 'Great White', used to pomp and ostentation: shrewd colonial that he was, he knew when to leave the cane-fields for the drawing-room.

Marie de Lériv danced her first quadrille without gusto. She seemed quite reserved. Then she was carried away by a certain Chevalier de la Tempétueuse, who had the audacity to sweep her off her feet! After this bit of high-flying, the Marquis de Pett, proud descendant of the Dutch Jew Peter, who had given his name to the capital, Port-à-Peter, later Pointe-à-Pitre (perhaps the *Pitt*, enclosures ringing cock-fights, derives from this man's name?), came to pay respect and solicit the favour of a dance. Unluckily, or luckily, at the same moment the Lord de Saint-Houël introduced himself, bowing low, with a gush of ingratiating words — all the tralala of the *ancien régime*. He was a classic aristocrat and Marie never imagined she would live to meet such an idiot. The Marquis de Pett had already horrified her. Without so much as a by-your-leave, abandoning Pett and Houël, she marched to the orchestra, seized a violin, tucked it under her chin, and launched into a beguine.[1] After a moment of astonishment, the young men delighted in the small revolution she had effected. They literally tore girls from their mothers' sides and out on to the slippery parquet. They had found an outlet for their long suppressed energy, throwing good manners to the wind. Every hot-blooded young man present praised and acclaimed her. This Marie de Lériv hadn't seated herself demurely at the piano, as she might have done; as if to underline her scorn for their society she had snatched up a violin.

The Count frowned. What's this? Marie! His daughter in the orchestra, and playing a beguine on the violin! The 'Great White' stifled the involuntary cry he was about to utter. This wouldn't do at all, it must stop. For the moment, however, he had to bow before the immense success his daughter was enjoying. Supple-waisted, she danced with partner after partner, her balance and timing so harmonious that the very air-waves seemed to animate them; she would then break off and go back to the orchestra to guide them through — first violin in a long dress. Effortlessly, she struck up on the fiddle, the piano and even the guitar, on which she tripped through some Spanish rhythms scarcely known in the country, like the 'Calypso' or the 'Calende'.

Bodies trembled under the pulse of roaring blood; small hands gripped wide shoulders, thin waists were gripped between strong hands; delicate feet jumped, impatient or joyful; skirts ballooned, settled back and swelled again, enveloping partners who tensed at the contact. Then came a tune whose troubling sweetness drew involuntary sighs. It annoyed some of the girls, who gave their partners the slip. Others were more agreeable, up to a certain point, but only the most forward blades imposed a *pas de deux*. Couples entwined and reeled about as if possessed of a single floating soul. Partners contemplated each other with rapture. Faces in which gratitude and mutual recognition were mingled at each step and turn expressed a strange life of their own, and sometimes there was a sweet confusion in their glances.

Marie was not only beautiful, but brimming with life and gaiety

[1] A dance which originated in the Antilles.

that set desires alight. What an overflowing of joy, since she had taken control of what was, in its fullest sense, 'her' soirée! Time whirled past. To seize the instant as it flew and be swept away to some miraculous new rhythm! Besieged by admirers, she never lost her head; she fended off the most persistent — even the Chevalier de la Tempétueuse — by returning to the orchestra and taking it in hand with her bow when she felt hemmed in. Perpetually alert and alive, she exerted a sway over men and events that astonished the Count himself.

In her enthusiasm she excelled — interpreting or improvising a new tune, or on the dance floor inventing new steps with her young legs, swivelling hips and palpitating breasts. Her dream was one of pure pleasure. She desired a place without horizon, untrammelled by sea or mountains, so she could go everywhere playing music and dancing.

Who would have believed a girl of eighteen would behave like this? The Count resolved to look severely on those high spirits of hers. It was crucial that he keep his sang-froid and remain calm at this turn of events. But the problem remained: how was he to come to terms with his child, whom he had sent to France — to Paris itself — so that she might receive a polished education, and who had come home a woman, visibly the mistress of herself and already in advance of her age and its traditions? To strike up a beguine in his own house! He was afraid she might go too far.

The negroes on Vallet were left wondering.

What on earth was going on at Durivage? Something more than a good harvest, that much was sure. When sugar-cane is pulped and shredded, one can deduce how many barrels of 'resin' it will make from the number of waggons that transport it to the mill. Close neighbours can likewise calculate how many tons of white sugar will be crystallized and, when resin is cooked to obtain what is known as 'battery-syrup', whether it will be used for distilling tafia, vintage rum at 56°, or industrial varieties. Not a bottle escapes the avid curiosity of those who speculate whether the rum will be 'white-grape' — which is left to mature naturally into vintage rum — or 'house-rum' which has to be drunk within the year as punch. A good harvest is common knowledge. . . . So what *was* going on at Durivage, to explain the presence of so many young men, and all those berlins unloading so many fabulous girls on to the lawns of the residence? Above all, who was the wizard playing the outlandish music that triggered such frenetic applause? What was happening in the house of the Béké, who was already marked for death and whose ancestor, the Red Corsair, had shipped so many slaves to Guadeloupe?

The negroes on Vallet watched and listened the whole night through. During this season the tropical sky streams with stars, their yellow trails lit up by a great lantern moon that seems to hang within reach. Its light bathed the couples, and picked out every tree. Palms that stood like sentinels guarding the flowering lawns seen from an angle looked like cathedral columns. Where else can you find such graceful boles? More modestly, the coconut-trees dangled their mouth-watering fruit within the shadow of their manes. Not a leaf stirred; the Atlantic winds were blowing elsewhere. The *filaos* scarcely dared to join their song to the new music. The negroes were all ears, burning to know who could play like that. But despite the clearness of the night, the shining of a thousand candles, petrol lamps, and torches made of burning tow, despite even the flames thrown up by brands of dried cane-trash, they did not see the fairy-fingered girl who sent a new shiver through their souls. But O'Dingue and Tonton-Hubé, dressed for an evening after work in corsair breeches and jerkins, exchanged knowing glances and retired, apparently to bed.

By morning, of course, the negroes on Vallet and elsewhere knew what had been going on; but no one ever knew exactly what O'Dingue and his younger brother did when they slipped like cats through the gardens of Durivage, nor what they observed in the Béké's house and why. What pact did they agree between themselves?

Indeed, what those two did see is perplexing enough: with the guests gone and the lamps extinguished, the Count just stared at his daughter without a word. He behaved like a perfect stranger. Yet he had no one except her. For a long time he had looked forward to her return from Paris to adorn Durivage with her presence, to bathe in the reflected glory of being able to offer the richest young men in the country at her feet. For an heiress to marry an heir was, in the Creole tradition, quite proper. But he had not envisaged such a quick triumph — and triumph it was! So he fixed his daughter, his only daughter, with a sober eye; her mother had died bringing her into this world, and he would have done anything for her, would still do anything for her, his own flesh and blood. His very *raison d'être* for the last eighteen years as he laboured to beautify Durivage had been this sole descendant of the Red Corsair, and he contemplated her darkly.

That was the scene the 'false-twins' observed through a window of the great reception hall of Durivage. Then Tonton-Hubé signalled to O'Dingue and the intruders vanished, as they had appeared, subtle as cats. And no one ever knew what words were exchanged, or what pact was made between them as they returned to Vallet by a long detour through the Grands-Fonds.

Shackle beauty at your peril!

After this memorable evening, Marie was escorted not by the customary 'Nanny' but by a chaperone — a dragonish old maid, a distant relative who had run the household since the death of Marie's mother. As a consequence the girl could visit only a handful of carefully selected friends.

Most of her days were spent playing the violin or the piano, reading works of a philosophical nature or travel books pronounced wholesome and inoffensive after a scrupulous examination by an ecclesiastical censor. She liked best to walk (chaperoned of course) to the west of Durivage, along the shore of the sea-water lake called Bridelle, a long arm of water between a rampart of rock and a pearly cove full of swallows. The poet has sung of this beach:

> On sand milled finer than a diamond's dust
> A glaucous sea rocks emerald and returns
> In sighs sunk deeper than a young god's lust
> Leaving the shoreline dressed in foaming flecks.
>
> The molluscs dawdle in the lighted deep:
> Swimming upwards the frail needlefish
> Break the surface in a soundless leap
> And fly on past, flashing transparent wings.
>
> The sea-snails cling to the granite blocks;
> The eels hide submerged in holes;

> There is algae on the pearl and pearl in rows
> That shake out fire, a million flakes.

Every night a black siren came to call her lover, a slave who had
been slaughtered there like a lamb. Marie would listen for the
siren's song mingling with the screams of the victim, and fill her
lungs with great gulps of salt air. It was a troubled but exquisite
expectation, rewarded by the stuff of dreams.

On Sundays and feast-days the whole family took a carriage and
drove to mass at the town of Sainte-Anne. In church, she played
the pedal organ and sang the 'Deo Gracias'.

There were no more dances — one a year was the limit — and
the rest of the time she was enclosed by the monotonous
conventions that hemmed in her youth.

But an artist cannot be shut away like that for long. Shackle
beauty at your peril.

It is a fact of history, proven and inevitable. How, then, did she
manage to escape the network of surveillance and join in the
Antillean night-life, the foil to the day's artificialities that were
paraded before the eyes of the world to maintain the myth of white
moral excellence? How did she avoid the gimlet eyes of the
scandal-mongers? Or attune herself to the tropical magic where

> Vast and flashing, the limpet night
> Clings to the lines of silent hills
> In the pearl and coral clouded cold
> Of a wide sky-window, phosphor bright.

In silk jacket and trousers, with dancing shoes on her feet, violin
tucked under her arm and one of those curious broad-brimmed
cane hats on her head, crammed with blond curls, she would
vanish into a small covered tilbury driven by an enigmatic
coachman, a large, comical negro who was something of a skirt-
chaser and drinker. She was still under the protection of this
discreet and massive silhouette when he drove her, as dissatisfied
as before, back to the parental cloister. Then, in the close silence of
her room, she would fall asleep, and her face would relax into its
childlike beauty.

Shackle beauty at your peril . . .

Who could have guessed that the young and talented Countess
with the angelic face, who played Bach on the cathedral organ of

Sainte-Anne during the Sunday service, was the same as the tomboy who played diabolically syncopated beguines in a brothel? To be sure, the Homecoming Ball had excited public curiosity. The Chevalier de la Tempétueuse had friends as fiery as himself. Moreover, all the negroes around Durivage had pondered long on what they had seen, or thought they had seen in the moonlight. It was quite clear that this white girl could not be a 'pure' white, playing those beguines as she did. Her independent disposition allowed her to dismiss her chaperone with a few well-chosen words; she could even meet her father's eye without flinching. She still dedicated whole days to playing piano works unknown in the Antilles: Mozart, Mendelssohn, Chopin, but they all took on a new syncopation.

She was a brilliant violinist, able to attack and develop a Paganini-style cadenza and then modulate into a glissando with the same impeccable mastery. Notes strung out on rhythm poured from her Stradivarius. Was it *she* who played nightly in the red-light district?

Certain fortunate people shared her intoxicating secret, but trumpeting it abroad would have brought down the worst on her. From time to time the local newspaper reported that a certain Marquis de la Braguettière had been seriously wounded by the Chevalier de la Flamberge in a duel over a heroine whose identity remained mysterious. The Chevalier de la Tempétueuse himself was found one morning barely alive in a field. There was no doubt about it: he had been flogged. By whom? His friends advised him not to try to find out if he valued his life. It was perilous to betray the secret of Marie de Lériv. But did anyone benefit from obliging her by keeping it?

The same astounding girl knew how to defend herself, and for a woman she was dangerously gifted in this difficult art. Those who tried to force their attentions on her found to their cost, and too late, that her violin bow was more effective than a sword: one spirited thrust and *voilà*! it plunged straight into her aggressor's right eye. She could hold her own, cruelly: there was nothing she couldn't grasp, nothing she couldn't parody. The changing aspirations of her heart and thought had no other purpose than to prevent her from becoming the voluptuous plaything of her nocturnal companions.

One day, or rather night, on the road from Pointe-à-Pitre to Sainte-Anne, the police discovered a secret cabaret — the 'Club of the One-Eyed' — where a seething mass of well-born young men, totally naked and wearing patches over their right eyes, were dancing the bamboula without music, singing instead to the rhythm of their bare feet on the floor. The scandal was hot to handle . . .

At least once, the little wanton must have accepted the homage of one of her gallant and impetuous admirers, or else have failed to use her foil in time, since she became pregnant (no deftly flattered woman fails to fall) just when her father announced that arrangements had been satisfactorily concluded for her to take Lord Saint-Houël for husband.

The news left her bewildered, and she stared at her father without a word.

The Count continued, explaining that Houël, nobly born as he was, had been peculiarly demanding about the dowry, but in spite of this they had happily reached a mutual agreement.

'You know the one I mean; the young Marquis whose fortune is large enough to stand comparison with your own future wealth . . .'

Marie fled to her room.

Had woman ever been unhappier than she? Could it really be that a man she had barely glimpsed at her ball intended to marry her, and had even concluded the affair with her father without so much as consulting her? A man as demanding of his rights as he was noble of birth.

So she too had a 'market value' like everything else? What a wretched offer of happiness! With that bow-legged imbecile!

Not once had she even considered him a possible candidate.

'I would rather die than belong to him.'

And to cap it all, here she was pregnant!

Until this moment none of these problems had so much as crossed her mind. She stared unseeing into the middle distance.

'Little idiot that I am!'

She began to argue with herself.

'Am I a child who must obey? No! I would rather go to the devil if not God!'

It wasn't impossible that she would commit suicide, or develop a mystical vocation, which was the time-honoured alternative open to unmarried mothers in the Antilles.

The very thought of it, lasting the space of a heartbeat, made her pull herself together. She got her breath back and realized with perfect lucidity that, apart from death, flight alone could afford her shelter from her father's rage. Repeating an ancestral act, she snatched up some gold pieces, and with a bundle over her shoulder and her violin under her arm, she ran to the other side of the church and took refuge on Vallet bluff.

Shackle beauty at your peril . . .

Before she even got there, Tonton-Hubé intercepted her. He might have been expecting her arrival. With his magician's sixth sense, the mulatto bastard of the O'O clan happened to be just at the right place at the right time. As overseer responsible for the estate and its exploitation he roamed all over the place. Such complicity between a young lady of the highest aristocracy and this man who despite his natural pride was little more than a peasant of low birth seemed highly improbable. So he must have come across her quite by chance. But then anything was possible for this young romantic who lived her nights to the full. Who knows, she might have developed a secret passion for the enigmatic mulatto the day she first clapped eyes on him. There are many Island stories at least as fantastic as this one, and they frequently involve such unexpected complications.

Antillean women have always fallen into two distinct types. The first are gentle and peaceable, with the captivating charm that has characterized them for centuries and given rise to the myth of Creole languor. The others are full of passion, motivated by sudden outbursts of unselfconscious, instinctive feeling and always ready to be whirled into affairs that reveal the tigress in them. They willingly submit to society's most constraining customs and then, without warning, risk their honour for a mere infatuation. Could Marie now attain to the fullness of love as she had to that of hatred? Nothing troubled her about leaving the whites for the blacks.

The disturbing mulatto was just where he should have been, to take her, bundle and all, gently into his arms. She didn't show the slightest resistance. He took her straight to O'Dingue, claiming to have found her in a corner of the forge, not far from the lake.

Apparently this came as a pleasant surprise to O'Dingue, who stood there a moment open-mouthed. Then he softened at the sight of the unhappy child. Heaven with its unfathomable designs seemed keen to bestow a rare favour on him. As he was obliged to accept this gift, he would do so come what may; quickly recovering the vivacity which earned him his surname 'the Mad', he had it proclaimed that Marie de Lériv was from now on under the protection of the black race of the Antilles.

At this time such words still caused a stir. From Pointe-à-Pitre to Basse-Terre, by way of all the towns and communes, little black flags showing the skull and crossbones could soon be seen flying on the houses of black planters and shopkeepers. The news drifted across the Caribbean, and shortly the sinister emblem appeared in Martinique. Soon a special envoy arrived from San Domingo to convey that larger island's admiration to O'Dingue. They were glad to learn that Guadeloupe would at last gain its independence, just as O'Makendal had predicted for all the Antillean Islands. O'Dingue put this approval to good use: he arranged several cargoes of arms, purchased at a good price with sound money.

There were terrible rumours in the air. Was a revolution really going to break out in Guadeloupe and beyond, all for the sake of a mere girl? History is full of such stories. What was to be done?

Clad in a long navy-blue jacket, a large bow-tie like a pair of wings, and with a top-hat on the back of his head, the giant negro — nearly two metres from top to toe — O'Dingue in person, entered the General Council, annihilating at a glance the few Békés still sitting there.

He saw them already skewered. Vengeance is all. He was always ready to leap to the defence of the former underdog, the fine black race which had been persecuted with such execrable perseverance. His grievance? The marketing of negroes. He acted in emulation of Bissette who, as early as 1830, had advised the slaves to keep themselves armed and secretly to lay in supplies, claiming that insurrection was the highest of duties.

For his part, Count de Lériv clenched his teeth and stared coldly back at his enemy. He knew very well that since the coloureds had been granted social and political rights, they thought of only one thing: slaughtering the Békés. Hadn't the black Haitians already refused those very same rights to *their* former masters? The General Council had to be cleared of all these negroes; for them, the

Republic meant lawlessness and the right to indulge in pure self-interest. The state of morale currently reigning in the country would undoubtedly lead to the most appalling catastrophe if due care were not taken.

The two antagonists thought only of themselves, without a single detached thought for the higher principles involved: the horror of racial prejudice, universal justice and equality before the law.

Every day the Count's faction awaited orders to go in and sack the Vallet residence. But it became clearer and clearer to the proud descendant of the Red Corsair that the negroes were just waiting for that signal to start a revolt in which he would be outnumbered three to one. The forces of public order could do nothing against the obvious numerical superiority of their enemy, not only in terms of men but of arms, which schooners unloaded nightly to the Vallet side of Sainte-Anne, not far from Durivage itself. This family affair would take a tragic turn; but as a man of caution, the Count bided his time.

Meanwhile, there was no shortage of minor incidents. A young Béké who entered Vallet on the quiet, in the wild hope of recapturing Marie, was quickly picked up by Tonton-Hubé and sent packing minus a few teeth, extracted by the usual method: forge tongs.

Before dismissing the young nobleman, who was nursing his jaw, the mulatto addressed him thus:

'*Yo bô avi: voyé bân mwé d'aut'e Békés, alosse zot ké fêt clib djol pas dents acwelmân, kuhwi! . . .*'

(I'll give you some good advice: send me more Békés like you, and you'll soon be able to found a 'Club for the Toothless'! And now, get out of here!)

From this quip, some people drew the conclusion that the 'magician' was perhaps familiar with Marie de Lériv's famous bow-thrust, executed against assailants who would later forget their affliction in the 'Club of the One-Eyed'.

THE 'Master of Forges' was called O'Balou le Balourd.

He scarcely ever left his workshop, content to turn wheels and pull levers, repairing waggons, patching up rusty boilers, straightening still-supports and shoeing horses, forever working iron or copper in an apotheosis of dull red glows exploding into showers of sparks, to the rhythm of heavy hammering and the wheezing of the forge bellows; no, he almost never left this infernal atmosphere. But when, by ill-luck, he found himself outside this sanctuary of intermittent lights and muffled noises, the shrewd pyromancer — who possessed wide practical know-how, and was one of the best mechanics of the age — would lose self-control and go right off the rails, an object of terror to any he encountered. As a slave, like his younger brother O'Dingue, he had seen his negress tortured before his own wild eyes. To help runaway slaves she trafficked in amulets and the like, perhaps using the trinkets as good-luck charms for the runaways. Pronounced a witch, she was burnt alive like Joan of Arc. Nothing was made of so ordinary an occurrence; after all, she was only a black woman. But her wretched screams as good as deafened O'Balou. And because he heard nothing, he said nothing, like a mute. Then he became a blacksmith. A blacksmith so that day and night, year after year, he could cut, break and shatter the chains that had bound his companions, tirelessly handling the tongs, iron, fire — all the tackle and trim of that domain. By the red light of the coal he often dreamed strange things. Even after Emancipation, when his brothers appointed him Master of Forges, by the coal that flared up and died down, bright red back to dull red, following the rhythm of his own breathing, he still seemed preoccupied. So long as he stayed within his forge — the biggest on Grande-Terre, to which factories outside the Vallet area sent machinery for repair — O'Balou found an outlet for his hatred by feeding the furnace with sack after sack of coal; by heating the metal on the platform and then seizing it with his tongs; by placing it straight on the anvil and working it, bending and fashioning it with the short sharp strokes

of a large hammer that beat out a tom-tom rhythm as he shifted
from foot to foot. With a huge smile on his lips he liked to imagine
that he held right there in front of him, on the anvil and under his
hammer, one of his wife's murderers. What a dream! To impale a
Béké on a spit, roast him above the forge, and when done to a turn
to put him under the hammer and flatten him, stretch him, turn
him over and then heat him up again, still on the spit, before
setting to work with the hammer again. What a vision! By reducing
all thought to one tragic obsession, a simple man can easily turn
into a monster. O'Balou became a blacksmith to avenge himself,
fire for fire, on those who had burned his friend. He cultivated
flames around him. Like a poor soul whose torment exalts his
hatred, he was perpetually meditating his revenge, hitting the
anvil with strong, clean strokes. He struck strong and clean on the
anvil, with the same measured stroke. What a stroke! What a
measure! And how it rang out! Men who spend their days in a forge
are always thirsty, which is hardly surprising. So O'Balou drank
long at work, if only to sustain his rhythm. The hammered iron
stammered out prayers. But the moment the Master of Forges left
his hell, his face shiny with running sweat and his eyes bloodshot
and rolling in their sockets, he would plunge forwards in a straight
line, smashing everything in his way. In the fresh air, he became a
drunken lunatic. Disdaining sword and pistol — although he
forged the former and repaired the latter — he engaged in hand-to-
hand combat, seizing those who blocked his way or happened to
cross it, giving them a good thrashing and trying to drag them back
to the forge.

It was true, he had gone a little out of his mind, and for the most
part his brothers stopped him leaving the forge, condemning him
to work there without respite, practically chained to the anvils,
unless they themselves needed him to settle some small account.
They spoke to him with their hands, using a secret sign language
invented by Tonton-Hubé — the simple-minded were convinced
the mulatto had created those diabolical signs — and having first
offered him some vintage tafia from the ancestral reserve, they
would unleash him on their prey. Like some great bear, O'Balou
would seize the appointed victim, strip him in classic style, hoist
him on to his wide shoulders and set off for the forge. But scarcely
had he got underway than he would drop his burden and begin to

cry like a child, for in his maddened imagination he saw his friend expiring in the flames. And then the poor devil would hurtle as fast as possible towards the lights to deliver his negress and find himself, as if by chance, before his furnaces. In sending him this vision God favoured him, because it protected him against crime; in spite of his fearful intentions, he had never committed murder. To have O'Balou beat you up might not be pleasant, but the consequences were slight. His brothers knew that.

Many stories circulate about this singular blacksmith. Slanderous tongues said it was he who, in 1871, set fire to the town of Pointe-à-Pitre in order to roast the white inhabitants.

'How do you know?'

'Why wasn't he arrested?'

The crime smacked more of O'Dingue, who thought that burning a town was always worth the trouble — it drove out the rats.

It took a scheming brain to choose the day a great festival was being held by the Békés, at an hour when several hearths were alight, which enabled the fire to take on such a catastrophic dimension the very moment the Governor was opening the evening ball. Certainly O'Balou was to be seen that evening, running here and there through the flames, but only to smother that element so familiar to him and above all to go to the rescue of many ladies, especially beautiful Creoles, who later offered him their tender thanks. One might be white, but a woman is a woman after all.

Other stories concerning the Master of Forges relate that certain persons, from the highest ranks of society, adopted this bear as an escort — a ruse which enabled them to arrive safely at their romantic rendezvous and rest assured of his protection and discretion — the man being deaf and dumb, redoubtable in combat and, in memory of his negress, chaste as a castrated monk. After their love-feasts, the beautiful ladies would ply their guardian angel with rum. The next day, O'Balou was to be found in a cane-field, otherwise known as the Vineyard of the Lord, ready to thrash the first Béké who came by, lift him on his shoulders and bear him off to his forge; but soon he would let his burden drop, and blinded by tears would run helter-skelter towards his furnace where he thought he could see his negress struggling through the flames. The vast forge threw out an intense heat, and the ghostly reality of that human torch appeared to his spirit like a river running upwards; the red feet fixed to the faggots formed its source, and streaming up the whole writhing body, it took flight in a white light that mingled with the beams of the rising sun. He saw that beloved form rise towards a resplendent heaven, grow beyond all measure, and stretch out her hands to shower a blessing on all the slaves. Then O'Balou got down on his knees and prayed.

Among his victims was the Chevalier de la Flamberge, whom some nameless beauty could not dissuade. O'Balou, a ferocious protector, felled the young fool, intending to drag him to the edge of his grill. In the darting brightness of the hot coals the negro was about to appease his strange desire when the woman, with a glint of malice in her eye, incited him instead to roll the young noble in the dust, and rub his entire body in it, offending parts and all.

All for a joke of course, and what a joke! The Guiablesse[1] and her grizzly got so carried away with the game, that the young man had to stay a long time near the sulphur pools of the Soufrière before he could get clean. But the spicy joke had an unforeseen result: in his efforts at ablution the noble discovered the miraculous properties of the sulphur or 'yellow bath'. The Chevalier was known to have a bad complexion, often spotty or marked by sinister stains; but no sooner had he plunged into the sulphurous water than his cheeks became pink as a girl's. And many others, as marked as him and worse, thus found their cure.

---

[1] A feminine sprite of great beauty, with one animal and one human foot. Like the sirens, she attracts men by her beautiful singing on moonlit nights and lures them into the forest, where they get lost.

WHILE Guadeloupe passed through one of the strangest crises in its history — the confrontation between the de Lerivs and the O'Os, graver in its way than that between the Montagues and the Capulets — a further provocation came in the form of a new curé. He had been posted to Sainte-Anne[1] and was rumoured to be massively strong, a sort of Graeco-Roman champion who had never met his match in Europe, or anywhere else for that matter. Because of this the Hierarchy, in its noble wisdom, thought him just the man to bring calm to the rival families, and put a stop to O'Balou's protection of unfaithful women.

All scandals had to stop. Too many tears had been shed, and too many homes destroyed. An act of penitence was in order.

The bigots welcomed the new priest like a Messiah.

However little commerce one may have had with a dyed-in-the-wool Antillean, it soon becomes unhappily clear that they are the most impossible of God's creatures. From his very first mass, Father Magloire was put to the test.

It was 28 July 1886, Saint Anne's feast-day. The inhabitants of the town spare nothing to honour their patron saint. Elaborate preparation is always in order. Everyone slaughters cattle, cooks cassava, breaches barrels of rum. Everything is prepared, especially blood-sausage, real black blood-sausage made with pure pig's blood, chives and pimento. Just get your teeth into that! Then, dressed as for Sunday, the people start out for mass, and take a vow of fasting.

Strange, remote 'peasant' negroes, with high wide shoulders, come with their herds from the furthest pastures; thick-set herdsmen, the colour of nutmeg, drive their cattle straight into the slaughterhouses; others bring headless calves and snorting mares. Riding fiery stallions, the Békés lead thoroughbreds by the bridle, the future spoils at fantastic auctions. Cows, kids, pigs and sows,

---

[1] Sainte-Anne is the largest borough in Guadeloupe, and is called the 'granary' of Grande-Terre.

all varieties of piglet arrive in scattered groups. And here come bulls from Trinidad, fortunately hobbled, though during one such fête, even that precaution didn't stop one of them from breaking its rope and charging the crowd. There are asses' colts — little red donkeys — saddled with foodstuffs, and handcarts which queue up in front of the stalls erected around the main square that extends from the church to the beach. There are stampings, cluckings, lowings, brayings, mingled with calls, cries and yappings shrill enough to burst the eardrum.

It's a great day, when people laugh and play like unrestrained children.

Here come the serving maids, carrying on their heads big trays of vegetables and fruit. Clad simply in brightly-coloured dresses or quilted wraps that fall from the neck to the feet, with a flap taken up and tucked in at the waist to allow their naked legs perfect freedom of movement, they move about like those Greek maidens at sacred feasts. Other beauties wear dresses and scarves of crimson, yellow, blue, bright green, lilac, violet, pink, and large cylindrical ear-rings and splendid necklaces with three, four or even five strings of golden beads. Some tall coloured men, very proud and well-bred, nobility in their very gait, grasp a fighting cock firmly in one hand, his comb on fire, and swing a cutlass in the other. Should you jostle them or jeer at the colour of their skin, which varies from black to brownish-yellow and includes all the tones between, you must be prepared to defend yourself. They are all varieties of mulatto, including quadroons, redheads, gryphons, sacatras and marabouts, and anyone who dares pass judgement on them or the quality of their fighting cock would be bloodied in open court. Whole fortunes can change hands thanks to the performance of those volatile birds in the 'pit', as belligerent in disposition as their keepers.

Eager children mix with the crowd. Some of them carry pretty cages, frames and bars made of sugar-cane cuttings and the nerves of coconut leaves, hence their lightness. Often ornamental, they are filled with red, insolent parrots and rainbow-coloured song-birds. Other urchins sing the praises of their 'castle':

> Come see my castle
> Magic for nuts,

> Cakes and beauty
> In the Prince's hut.
> Come see the Devil's wife
> Two sous for her Highness,
> Love and lightness
> As the day is bright.

The refrain is appalling:

> In my glass
> You see a miracle;
> On my 'pecker'
> You reach the pinnacle! . . .

This 'castle' is a sealed wooden soapbox in which, through a small aperture, one can admire either the fairy décor of Sleeping Beauty or some pornographic horror. These magical visions are paid for in acajou nuts and marbles. The children wander through the crowd, singing and playing castanets or the flute. If it weren't for the colour of their skin, they could easily be those small angels come down from the elegant cathedral tower of Sainte-Anne.

Acrobats perform on the grass, dancers show off on high stilts, strolling fiddlers and banjo players tune up and bohemians tap and shuffle tarot packs. The sellers of accras[1] are there, as well as those vending coconut milk, different coloured syrups, ices, sinobol — whipped ice sprinkled with mint or black-currant syrup — not to mention those with rum. It's not in fact a market, but everything is available. On the beach, fishermen lay out a variegated selection of fish, while others on the quayside fix a greasy pole over the sea. This pole, with a few tasty scraps hurled in alongside, attracts sharks.

The feast of Sainte-Anne is a happy one, part fair, part carnival and part bazaar. People come from a long way off, as much to try and sell something as to show off their wares, and above all to enjoy themselves. Competitions are organized; horse-racing, donkey derbys, hand-to-hand combat, wrestling and boxing, sword and sabre duels — some contestants seek an adversary to teach them the famous O'O thrust. The negroes of Sainte-Anne were the first to show the whites that d'Artagnan was outmoded. But by far the

[1] Cod fritters.

most popular spectacle is that of children from eight to twelve years old fighting against the sharks to win the title of 'Holô King'; that is, to be crowned in all solemnity and proclaimed the most adept at leaping out of the water, having delayed until the terrible jaws were almost upon him.

The day is a continual buzz from morning till night. First, however, everyone leaves his goods and surges into church. Before the sales by shouting, American-style auctioneering, different competitions and fiesta, the people must go to mass.

O'Dingue and Tonton-Hubé got wind of the bishop's intentions; Father Magloire had been charged with 'taming' the Saintannese.

Escorting O'Balou, the two 'compères' arrived unnoticed in front of the church when mass had already begun. They entered the porch, and at the very moment of the elevation, they let the Master of Forges loose in the nave. No one knows what they said to O'Balou in their secret language of sign and gesture, nor how many tipples of punch they plied him with. The giant walked straight up to the altar, just like that, without a word, without the slightest noise, a great ill-licked bear rolling his shoulders and buttocks, his hundred-kilo weight of muscle tensed by willpower into muffled vibrations. Delicately lifting his paws, he crept up on the priest who had his back turned to him and was at that moment raising the chalice towards Christ.

Heads bowed, the parishioners waited with great concentration for the accomplishment of the Eucharistic mystery. All the Békés were there, and an even greater number of negroes; all those who mistrusted one another and who, heads lowered, watched out of the corners of their eyes while meditating and praying; all working out their revenge, lightened with the hope that their sins and crimes would be pardoned — those already committed and those of the future. Confession is less for what one has done than for what one intends to do, and Saint Anne, the all-benevolent mother who was able to pardon Mary's original sin, so tenderly and mysteriously presented, would surely absolve them too. There were many present who lived by the sweat of their brows and who prayed: 'Give us this day our daily bread, and lead us not into temptation of the flesh — this being the only temptation really open to them. It was this, too, that Father Magloire wanted most of all to stamp out, but despite his herculean strength he could not do it because its consummation must happen for ever and ever, the Lord having said: grow and multiply . . . so be it.

In that second of luminous silence, spirals of incense rose up to welcome Christ.

A few heads looked up when O'Balou seized the priest by his shoulders and whirled him round; the gaping altar boys trembled with their handbells. When the first shock had passed, they witnessed Father Magloire pour the contents of the sacred vessel right on to O'Balou's bewildered face, and wrap him from head to foot in his sacerdotal vestments. The negro found himself in an awkward position; the wine from the chalice — if not the Lord's blood itself — had blinded him, and his legs were tangled in liturgical cloth. He fell to the floor and writhed in desperation. Magnanimously, Father Magloire watched him at his feet, like St Michael with the devil finally at his mercy.

But O'Balou managed to extricate himself from his sacred bonds, stood up and confronted his adversary. The struggle began.

At first, the church choir formed the ring. Some parishioners snickered, a small group looked on scandalized, while the majority divided smartly into two camps. Their passions were expressed under the mild gaze of the crucified, who seemed to writhe on his cross. The general shouting grew loud, died into isolated cries, then started up again even louder.

It was a splendid fight, the kind of sacrilegious spectacle it is good to watch from time to time. The antagonists were fairly matched, and as neither gained the upper hand the struggle went on down the entire length of the nave. Everything was overturned, as if a cyclone had passed, and the fight continued on the church steps, in the square[1] and finally in the fields. Which one would submit before a maddened crowd? Some wagered that the priest would thrash the negro. Others raised the bidding by swearing that the negro would 'devour' the priest. The betting varied according to the ups and downs of the fight. Friend mingled with foe, inciting the two colossi with cries of 'may the best man win!' The wretched police were not strong enough to separate the adversaries; they didn't even try since the spectacle was so good.

---

[1] The Place d'Armes, where more than one heroic combat has taken place.

They contented themselves with keeping back those who didn't leave the wrestlers enough space. As for the latter, they were either pinned to the ground or standing upright, engaged in a grotesque kind of waltz.

O'Balou wanted to guide the priest towards his forge and roast him. The priest struggled to drag his foe towards the beach and throw him to the sharks. And each understood the intentions of the other. They went one way, then the other. 'The good people' of Guadeloupe, especially the women, hoped the priest would resist, since they knew, those tender souls, that if he did, O'Balou would go wild, drag him off to his furnaces and roast him. Feminine logic, implacably rigorous as usual. These good ladies knew perfectly well that when they yielded to O'Balou he became humble and submissive, sweetly devoted to their charms. At the same time, he lost all his strength and wept in a heart-rending way; they could then manipulate him at will. Resisted, however, he became dangerous and invincible. This priest, who refused to concede defeat, would doubtless meet his end on a spit, bravo!

O'Dingue and Hubert foresaw the danger. O'Balou might easily turn wild, and no one could master him then. Father Magloire, human stupidity incarnate, didn't seem to realize he had to submit. The whole thing might turn nasty. Stage a farce and it turns into tragedy. The truth of the matter was that O'Dingue merely wanted to give the curé a warning, issued to churchmen in general, to mind their own business. But taunt a madman to accomplish it, and you risk going beyond the point of no return. O'Dingue and Tonton-Hubé looked once at each other, as they always did when they had an important decision to take, and, as always, understood each other's meaning without a word or gesture between them. The two cats leapt into the arena, delivered a volley of punches to the head, directed at the curé and O'Balou alike, and felled them both, out for the count on the grassy carpet, while the crowd looked on, not daring to utter so much as a hostile murmur.

These two excited O'Balou, and they now calmed him down.

A good soul attended to Father Magloire.

And the feast-day went on.

There is more to say — but what hasn't been said about this 'post-Emancipation' period? — that there was a fête every day, a ball every night and brawls at all hours. It was a period at once dramatic and a taste of things to come, when negroes no longer held back from fighting the whites in the streets. They even carried their women off into the depths of the woods, and later sent them home happy. Now there was no obstacle to a Béké marrying a proud velvet-eyed negress, and as a result the mulattos became fully accepted. Everyone was seized by a frenzied love of life, and gave themselves over to wild excitements. As for the curés who wanted to curb all that, they too have their part in these stories. There was Father Magloire, who thought he could 'tame' the Saintannese, and shortly after his arrival began by taking on a deaf-mute negro; yes, but *that* particular negro was called O'Balou, Master of Forges, and such things as had never been seen in the country took place before a rejoicing people.

Here is one episode in the contest between O'Balou and Father Magloire.

The curé of Sainte-Anne made enquiries about the deaf-mute negro. Who was he? How did he come by his double handicap? — and all sorts of questions about his family. He even went so far as to dig up information in the parish archives. This newcomer to the islands was capable of seizing a bull by the horns and overturning it on to the grass; and with it all he was very shrewd, intelligent, more crafty than Father Labat, whose natural successor he obviously was.

One day, Father Magloire tucked in his soutane and decided to pay O'Balou a visit.

He entered the Vallet estates and reached the edge of the dark lake, where he was astonished to see a blue flame-tree that seemed to laugh at his approach. In fact, the new curé did not believe in the famous miracle; he had been deceived quite enough already and was determined not to be taken in again by people who to amuse themselves at the expense of a newcomer would make up pretty well anything. But seeing that strangely welcoming leafy tree for the first time made him think. A laughing tree! It was a frightening phenomenon as well, possibly the work of the devil. In order to lift it from the realms of sensory illusion the tree must remain miraculous. Who knew whether he himself, humble Father Magloire, like Father Labat before him, was not a chosen instrument of God? This idea strengthened his determination and he went straight ahead towards the big forge, entered without knocking and planted himself in front of O'Balou. In one hand the negro was grasping a pair of tongs that held a molten horseshoe and in the other his massive raised hammer, ready to strike strong and clean on the anvil; it remained suspended before this unexpected visitor.

How did the priest get as far as here?

How did he escape the watchful Tonton Hubé? Did he still have all his teeth?

The very instant of his apparition a surge of flame lit up the whole forge.

Instinctively the apprentice blacksmiths took refuge like scolded children in the darkest corner of the workshop, a haven lit up by the whites of their boggling eyes.

Who was this archangel sent specially for the negroes?

The little round heads with crinkly black hair pressed against each other like balls packed in a box; it was impossible to count them, only their eyes and teeth were visible in the flickering shadow. When the great bellows blew on the brazier, light invaded every cranny, swamping those little stars in the corner and revealing faces among the cauldrons.

When he saw the priest in front of him, O'Balou froze, but he did so with dignity and without menace because he was on his own ground, in his forge, at the centre of his universe where he knew how to maintain an Olympian calm, be it in the very depths of hell.

'Hallo, O'Balou,' said Father Magloire.

'. . .!. . .'

'I have come to you, just as you came to me,' replied the curé.

O'Balou, of course, heard nothing and couldn't reply. Instead, he stared intensely at Father Magloire's lips. The latter quickly understood what that meant, and with complete naturalness began to speak with his hands, making the same cabbalistic signs as Tonto-Hubé, in that secret language — neither Latin, French nor Creole — unknown in the country.

This made the apprentices tremble all the more in their dark corner: what hellish jargon was this?

Father Magloire repeated his phrase, wordlessly. O'Balou showed that he understood by plunging the iron shoe into a water butt which went:

Plouf! . . . a-hi-hu! Ahii! . . . i! . . .
The hot iron, thrust into deep water, hissed and steamed:
Hihui . . . i!
Some white wisps of vapour rose gently from the trough and dispersed.
Finally the battle of fire and water was appeased.
The workshop grew darker, and was again flooded with light by a gust of air which came down the chimney. Even the wind was stuttering, witness to such a strange scene, made stranger still by the curé's gesticulations.
'I come,' went on Father Magloire, weaving the air with his hands, 'not from behind to seize you, which is what you did to me, for I am not one of those who uses surprise, no, I come to challenge you face to face.'
The phrases, well articulated by his hands and fingers, were clean and precise.
A sort of rumbling came from O'Balou's throat, and his hammer fell on to the anvil, bouncing several times:
Tita! . . . Tita! . . . Tita!! . . . Tatitati! Tatatita!
As if to get his hand in, the blacksmith tried his hammer on the anvil which, with a muffled sound, sang out in iambs and trochees.
And then his hammer began to speak. O'Balou moved it over the anvil, measuring out the strokes with gestures of his hand, gestures which became signs, hammering out syllables which corresponded to varying lengths of sound, the hammer dancing on the anvil and the anvil singing under the hammer. Father Magloire saw the words with his eyes, and heard the 'sound-signs' of the extraordinary speaking tom-tom:
'You lie, Curé, you lie Curé!'
The hammer spoke volubly, and with his other hand the blacksmith added punctuation and dotted his i's.
'Tita . . . tita . . . tita . . . you lie, Curé . . . you lie, Curé . . . you lie! I was no surprise to you, for you saw me coming, you saw my image in your lifted chalice, where I too saw myself, but too late. . . . As soon as I stretched my hands out to seize you, you turned round and poured the Lord's blood on my face, right in my eyes to blind me; then you wound me in your woman's clothes. . . . Tita . . . tita . . . tita. . . . Curé, you tricked me, and my escape I

owe to my ancestors . . . O'O helped me extricate myself . . .
tatita-ti . . . tata . . . tita . . . Baoum! . . .'

It spoke out with joy: Baoum!

The hammer was garrulous, supplying details, while the
enchanted anvil brightened the whole forge.

The little negroes began to giggle in their corner, because they
heard the joyful sound of the anvil without quite knowing what it
was jabbering about. For his part, O'Balou tapped out his
language with an almost delirious joy. And the curé understood
him perfectly.

He answered with his hands and fingers:

'Agreed! Agreed O'Balou . . . I saw you coming. But it was you
who wanted to deceive. . . . And can one really be a conqueror in
such conditions? O'Balou, think for an instant of the death which
comes to all of us, who are still full of sin! The Lord protected me,
as he protected you . . . but no more of that. Tell me, O'Balou, are
you really courageous?'

Baoum!

'Well then, listen to me carefully; I am Father Magloire,
champion of the two worlds, champion of Europe and America,
and I have come to meet my match in you. We shall have a unique
contest, the like of which no man has ever tried before . . .'

'Ababa! Ababa! Ababa! . . .' answered the hammer. 'Ababa!
Ababa! Ababa! . . . I am I, O'Balou, the strongest man in the
world; Europe and America are nothing to me, for I am the
champion of the whole Caribbean sea . . .

Ababa! Ababa! Ababa! . . . I am O'Balou, who heats iron until it
becomes as red as blood! . . . Ababa! Ababa! Ababa! . . . I am
O'Balou who drinks the blood of metal, not the blood that is wine!
. . . Ababa! . . . I eat the molten iron which gives me muscles of
steel! . . . Ababa! . . . I am the Master of Forges, the strongest man
on any Caribbean shore . . . Ababa! I am the Master of Forges, and
the Master of the Universe as well, I, O'Balou the blacksmith . . .'

'Calm down, my friend!'

Baoum! . . .

'Calm down, calm down!'

'Ababa! . . . Ababa! . . . I am O'Balou, bigger and stronger than
the Man of Iron; I am Hephaestos, master of forge and
metalwork!'

'Friend, you have a big mouth, but will you listen to my suggestion?'

'Baoum! Speak, Curé . . .'

'Here then is my idea. The strongest between us will be he who reaches the lake first with an anvil on his back! If you win, if you get to the edge of the lake before me, you can put me on a spit and roast me; if I win, for ten consecutive years you will have to carry the statue of Saint Anne on your shoulders in the annual procession we are going to organize . . . ten years of penitence are well worth my flesh for roasting, and it gives me time enough to alert Rome about canonizing your Chimène . . .'

In reply, the hammer was sent flying across the workshop, its trajectory broken several times by scraps of iron and hidden anvils which clattered as it hit them, leaving red gleams in its wake.

Chimène was the name of the negress who had been burned alive (in fact, Chimine, from the French 'chemin', the way). She was so named because her mother had given birth to her and abandoned her on the side of a road. What a fabulous black saint she might become! Had he been the strongest of the strong, he was unable now to be anything but the meekest. That was the catch.

The noise of the flying hammer was amplified by several echoes and became like thunder. The little negroes trembled against the wall. Once again, the flames flared up in a long exhalation that worked upon the fire, igniting everything that would burn. Everything was lit up, and every colour took on a reddish hue: pots became stars and cauldrons suns. Colours can sometimes speak as well, like the blacksmith's hammer.

And O'Dingue was there; Tonton-Hubé was there, with several negroes behind them, curious to find out what was going on in the master blacksmith's forge.

O'Balou was cast in the same mould as Balourd, since he too let himself be caught out by the curé, agreeing to run in the famous race and knowing that he had to lose it in the hope that his Chimène would one day be made a saint.

But has there ever been a black saint? The curé must have been employing all his faith . . .

O'Balou not only lost the stupid wager, but two anvils into the bargain: the curé's and his own. Father Magloire, who at thirty was by far the younger of the two, was the first to reach the edge of the lake, but he didn't have time to put down his burden since O'Balou, for all his sixty years, was hot on his heels. Whether he simply lost his balance, or was carrying out a last calculated manoeuvre worthy of an O'O, the negro ran straight into him and both of them went plunging into the lake with their mass of iron. It was then a matter of trying to drown the curé; but despite his tangled dress he managed to clamber out.

For years now, at the head of the procession that opens the feast of Saint Anne in Guadeloupe, O'Balou has borne the effigy of the Blessed Virgin's mother on his shoulders.

Will he hold to his ten years?

ANOTHER consequence of the event that overturned the whole country, of a more tragic nature, followed; Lord Saint-Houël, deaf to the entreaties of his family, the warnings of Father Magloire and the voice of experience, was stupid enough to send his seconds to O'Dingue.

The duel took place on Houëlmont, the extinct volcano windward of Basse-Terre which owes its name to Lord-Petit-Près, Saint-Houël's ancestor and governor of Guadeloupe from 1643, who purchased it from the West India Company along with Marie-Galante, la Désirade and les Saintes;[1] it was he also who captured the O'O of Saint-Martin, the one versed in the secrets of whitening sugar. Nothing was left to chance; it was to be a duel to the death. The seconds chose this spot because it is a long way from Sainte-Anne and would not be found by those intent on stopping the confrontation, in particular the police who had been alerted by the young nobleman's family. The duel wasn't simply a matter of defending a woman's honour; much else was at stake, on both sides, and ancestral hatred was at the bottom of it all. They wagered their lives on it. It was a waste of time trying to dissuade either party, too late to soothe their outraged pride.

O'Dingue was at the time considered the finest swordsman in all the Caribbean islands, but Saint-Houël had just returned from Paris where he had been trained by an internationally known master-of-arms. His friends rallied round as well, the swash-buckling Chevalier de la Tempétueuse among them, and helped him to reach top form during the week of negotiations and arrangements required by the code of honour. He had revised the parries to every possible surprise lunge, and sharpened his own fatal thrust. What no one knew is that O'Dingue had been counselled by his trainer Tonton-Hubé not to lunge at his adversary but to corner him on a small parapet at the end of a terrace of rock and then apply the O'O touch — worse than

[1] At the same time as the sale, du Parquet nabbed for himself Martinique, St Lucia, Grenada and the Windward Islands.

Jarnac's, and against which no parry, by its very nature, could be attempted.

Two groups of three riders each, three whites on one side, two negroes and a mulatto on the other, spent three consecutive days travelling about the island to shake off their pursuers. This revealed the determination on both sides, and each rider was armed to the teeth with swords and pistols.

It was dawn when they came to their final rendezvous. The extremely early hour added to the tragic mood. Rags of mist still hung between the sparse trees and a few leaves were wet with dew. Infrequent plants flourished in the red and undulating earth that is pocked in places and tinted pink.

O'Dingue knew every inch of ground as if it were Vallet itself with its great woods; indeed, he knew the whole country in the same sort of detail, having run all over it as a child with the mastiffs at his heels. No ex-slave can efface his early life, and the post-Emancipation negroes, whose moral sense was no less developed than their oppressors', were not generally disposed to forgiveness. O'Dingue had sworn that for the rest of his life he would make the whites pay for the sufferings they had inflicted. He had feelings he couldn't control; every time he saw a white he wanted to kill him. There was no possible conciliation. The most violent act was an insufficient expression of his passion, and a man like Saint-Houël could expect nothing from him. Hatred of this kind is a strange thing. Houëlmont is not very high and stands surrounded by other hills which with their peaks, humps and sugar-icing crests give Guadeloupe its rugged appearance. To the north lies the Soufrière range which bares a golden brow in the first gleams of morning. It is a rather muted landscape, austere and beautiful.

At the prescribed place and without unnecessary formality the two men drew their swords. The seconds stood on either side to follow the duel, ready with their weapons should anyone try and interfere.

The Chevalier de la Tempétueuse kept an eye on O'Balou. A slim, handsome youth of medium height, sword in hand with the proud face of a Béké, he reckoned he was more than a match for the black giant at his side. He had an account to settle after his unhappy adventure which had ended in the dust. There was no doubt of the part played by the Master of Forges in humiliating him, and the repugnant memory of it pursued him. At the first irregularity in the contest, he would puncture that gross balloon so that it collapsed once and for all. He snickered at the thought of it.

The Chevalier de la Flamberge was tall and slim, with thinning blond hair that fell over an angular face. Full of himself after a recent duel in which he had seriously wounded the Marquis de la Braguettière, he had still to avenge the loss of his right eye. He stood opposite Tonton-Hubé and promised himself that he would kill him: 'If that rogue so much as moves, I'll put out his eye!' The leer of his pursed lips revealed his private satisfaction.

The contest did not seem equal. O'Balou, the deaf-mute, did not hear the clash of swords and could only follow the play of steel with his eyes. He approved its temper like a connoisseur, and had he forged the swords himself he would doubtless have rigged Houël's so that it snapped. Out of the corner of his eye, he too kept unobtrusive watch on the Chevalier de la Flamberge, whose weapon wouldn't even graze his skin, tougher than a hippopotamus's. Indeed he resembled that curious river-horse, feature for feature, muscle for muscle, and possessed its appalling strength. A man of one hundred and forty kilos is a frightening phenomenon — as though he had a double set of ribs. This same monster was smiling blissfully at the tragic moment, picturing in his elementary way how the little Béké would be buttered with the flower of boiling sulphur.

Tonton-Hubé himself followed the duel attentively, without neglecting the two Chevaliers, and he kept a wary eye on O'Balou who might make a blunder. Before the event, he had taken the precaution of pointing out to the blacksmith that O'Dingue was in no danger and it was therefore useful to pick a fight with young Flamberge. When the affair was concluded, most probably by Houël being cleanly despatched to hell where he would join his ancestors, nothing further was to be undertaken except in legitimate self-defence; in that event, and in that event only, would he give him an exact signal, at which point O'Balou would fling away the sword for which he had no use, grasp his enemy's blade in his hand and for the rest, there were no holds barred. For his part, Tonton-Hubé knew how to disarm Flamberge, and thanks to his trusty pliers more than one tooth would fly. He was so certain of

victory, however, that all this seemed superfluous; he had
dispensed with the usual magical incantation and the vipers'
poison, specially imported from Martinique and spread on
O'Dingue's sword. Its effect was such that the slightest scratch
would paralyse the foe.

Houël faced O'Dingue and went on the offensive, imagining that
before daybreak he would wash his hands in blood and wipe away
the Béké's shame. Only honour, that concept to which the nobility
likes to reduce everything, requires that one risks one's life to take
another's.

The antagonists savoured a strange but exalting thing, a
persistent taste that made them dream: hate, livid hate, screaming
from its thousand sepulchres in their entrails.

Despite his age — he must have been in his fifties — O'Dingue
systematically steered the young lord, who was between twenty
and twenty-five, towards a crevasse. He drove him backwards, and
just as the disk of the rising sun sent up its quavery red columns
towards the heavens, his eyes staring straight into the eyes of his
victim and not leaving off until Houël looked away, he brayed,
screamed, belched:

'O'O! . . .'

In the horrified seconds that followed, time missed a beat; the
rash young man, surprised, blinded, off-balance, fell head-over-
heels into a crater of boiling sulphur.

The woods and the plain were silent.

The body of the wretched fellow was never recovered. Had the
terrain been less fissured this 'accident' might not have occurred.
But who knows what terrible fate O'Dingue would then have
reserved for Saint-Houël?

Though he received news of the outcome, Count de Lériv still
refrained from giving the order to attack Vallet.

After that day the Count's friends saw a big change come over him.
He seemed weary, tormented, lost in some private monologue;
vague ramblings, blurred suppositions, a darkness in his look,
would be followed by a sudden gesture of refusal made with his
hand. Shaking his head, his voice emphatic, he burst out: 'No! . . .
It isn't possible!'

Like his daughter, he remonstrated with himself.

'I must choose . . . choose what? . . . She has hidden a complete double life from me. Since when?'

Had anyone else managed to deceive him, wound his pride and deprive him of his vengeance, it would not have wrung him out to this degree.

Eventually, still deep in thought, he leapt on a horse and galloped up and down the fifty yards of public beach bordering Vallet. The cane-cutters grew tense as they watched him. It must be a lunatic!

Then Tonton-Hubé appeared, out of nowhere as usual, and put everyone back to work, apparently without worrying about the rider who had had the temerity to wander so far.

Ah! If only he could seize him, tear out all his teeth and hear him groan.

In fact, the Count's person was sacred: the order had been given never to harass him so long as he did not cross the perimeter of the property; if he ever did, he was to be spared and escorted back to his own estate.

The sight of that tireless rider passing back and forth in front of Vallet became common. They heard the galloping horse, saw it appear and draw close, thundering through the naked blue against the purple horizon; then the rider moved off, carried on by the speed after racing, and rode back along the beach, propped on his mount, dust hanging in his wake. He was mantled in white sand, like a ghost returning to its refuge.

In fact, force was never used against Vallet. Under the persuasive protection of Tonton-Hubé, in a richly exotic atmosphere, Marie de Lériv was able to develop her exceptional musical gifts at leisure.

In the evenings, O'Dingue with his family and a few friends gathered to listen to her clear, melodious voice sing love songs that evoked tender anguish and luminous vision. Her rising voice stirred the sombre depths inside each of them; the 'thread' of a brilliant run would make them hunch and tighten up inside, so that they could grasp it better; the returning melody released the tension, and they breathed again, excited by the triumph after flight. She seemed to grow pure of her faults, cleansing herself with sounds as tender as the tenderest and most exalting thoughts of love.

So what was going on at Vallet?

The servants crowded round the open doorway of the salon while beyond the veranda negroes from the fields sat on the grass. Even the passing stranger would stop, gaze, and listen, thinking himself transported into some mysterious waking dream.

Even Father Magloire was there, with O'Balou by his side, listening along with everybody else. While the priest had no chance of keeping his promise to sanctify Chimène, he had still worked a great miracle in restoring O'Balou's voice to him, and then his hearing — which he opened to the outside world, in particular to Marie de Lériv's music. While O'Balou listened, he would cradle himself in his arms and ceaselessly gesture with his hands, as if striking his great hammer on an anvil . . .

Even the whites from Durivage could hear. Something far more important than Emancipation had taken place; the negroes they had tried to load with chains and exploit were now singing and dancing!

On her violin, Marie de Lériv played the Creole tunes that had lulled her tenderest childhood as well as those she had composed herself, mingling European and African folk-tunes into the rhythm. Then she snatched up her Spanish guitar and strummed chords that flared like sunbursts in the dark. These musical evenings, during which O'Dingue's wife, the glossy-haired Indian, accompanied Marie on the piano, invariably ended with dancing in which joy mingled with perennial longing.

No doubt about it; Tonton-Hubé the 'magician' had captured a spirit for Vallet, even as it flew out of Durivage.

When Marie de Lériv gave birth to Anne, a beautiful *chabine*[1], the bamboula was danced non-stop for several days and nights all over Sainte-Anne, except perhaps at Durivage, where the gaunt owner was seen galloping tirelessly up and down the beach on his snorting horse.

No one knows at quite what stage the sombre death's-head, emblem of the O'O, was replaced by a small flag with black, white and yellow stripes — the new sign to distinguish descendants of the Black Corsair. Opposite Vallet, at Durivage, a red flag appeared to

[1] A white-mulatto cross, with sandy-red hair.

mark out the family of the Red Corsair.[1]

It made no difference to the cane-cutters of Vallet who still sang as they worked. From the impeccably polished factory spirals of steam rose gently above the lush countryside. When the coconut clusters began to turn from green to yellow and the flame-trees went red (except the one by the lake that remained an unmixed blue) it was good to follow the black milkmaid as she walked like a queen with an urn on her head, swaying her hips and breasts. She would be offered guava, and fruit from the marmalade-tree. Those who picked her a prickly pear had every chance of tasting its streaming purple juice on her lips. Couples dreamed at the lakeside. Red waves, shot through at times by tints of blue, seemed to rise from the green blades of grass and run along the watery savannah, revived by drawn-out sighs. Tonton-Hubé still tore out a few marauders' teeth from time to time, but he never disturbed the lovers entwined beneath the blue flame-tree.

[1] Marie de Lériv, never lacking in wit, later embellished the arms with a violin, flanked on the right by a bow and on the left by a sword.

ALL the while time was moving through generations that were similar — yet so different. Those whose passion had moulded spirit and brow had been succeeded by others who struggled to consolidate the earlier triumphs; and they in turn gave way to a pensive generation growing up to confront an inscrutable and disconcerting future. Looking back, the progress was a bloody one. Even the present seemed tainted with its cruel stains. But for all that, Moloch appeared to demand fewer and fewer victims, as if his thirst had been quenched. What colour would emerge on the horizon? Weren't they simply living in a lull between terrors? One thing was certain: century after century, here as elsewhere, the great joys and sorrows were forged by those who tried to elude a tragic destiny as much as by those who flung themselves blindly into it.

Often the song of the Stradivarius rose into the tropical night in which a slim, well-bred boy, black as the surrounding night and called Baindingue, eldest son of O'Dingue and the beautiful Indian, played in company of a little girl with brownish-yellow skin the colour of marmalade, eyes like almonds and long crinkly hair that was tinted slightly red like a true chabine's. The girl was Anne de Lériv, natural daughter of the Countess Marie de Lériv. These children bathed naked in the moonlit phosphorescence of the Antillean sea. Other children played around them; but these two were inseparable.

The violin sang out, accompanied by chords from a piano, while the two children played Holô, a ducking struggle in the water, as far as possible away from their brothers and sisters.

They grew up and were separated. Baindingue was sent to study law in Paris. His brothers, who were less intellectually gifted, were sent off on sailing-ships to learn about island-to-island trading — for the family's benefit, naturally — or were put under Tonton-Hubé who initiated them in forge and factory work. All the boys were dark; some were legitimate, others natural children got by O'Dingue on the local whores, although the Indian always treated them as her own. They were a gang of hooligans, as quarrelsome as each other, and women-chasers with it — like their father — though he seemed more settled since the arrival of Marie de Lériv. Only Baindingue, the future head of the family, seemed well-adjusted.

O'Dingue and Tonton-Hubé agreed that Anne should receive a polite education at the boarding-school reserved for daughters of the Békés. But only white girls were admitted to Versailles. The nuns called themselves religious and professed that all human creatures are equal before God, but as teachers they inculcated the opposite. 'They must be reformed!' exclaimed Schoelcher. 'Education must be perfectly equal and open to all; let parents stupid enough to want it otherwise keep their children at home and be responsible for their ignorance. That is what those with true principles must profess.'[1] Anne, a chabine, had a touch of the negro. The nuns knew it. Did they have the right to deny a particular race its future? Well, if they refused to take her, the school would be razed to the ground. At that, she was admitted with embarrassing haste by a mother superior. She had been terrorized by a visit from two ambassadors at the head of a train of negroes, armed with cutlasses, who gambolled about on thorough-breds the whole length of the Champ d'Arbault in front of the convent, waiting for their leaders to emerge. Marie de Lériv gave her consent, on condition that her daughter should not spend a single day in the metropolis. Thus her descendant never had the chance to discover Paris.

During the holidays, the pretty little Creole arrived home at Vallet like a whirlwind, flung off her dark uniform, donned a pair of corsair breeches, leapt on to the horse provided by Tonton-Hubé and galloped over the vast estate in search of this same Tonton who was in all places at once, cajoling the lazy and tending the wounded, whether man or beast; an indefatigable giant, so solitary and yet so active.

Towards her mother and Tonton-Dingue — she was often mischievous and dropped the prefix 'O — she behaved quite well, pretty much as a daughter should. But with Tonton-Hubé she gave her wild and roguish nature full rein, adoring this man both

[1] Actual letter from Schoelcher. From the archives of Jean-Louis Jeune.

rustic and refined, cruel and yet compassionate towards the misfortunes of others. She had a vague notion of his courage too, since she had been told long ago how before she was born he had saved her mother from certain death.

'Tonton' was the most handsome and gentle of men, though he would from time to time tear teeth out of gaping jaws, untouched by the shrieks of his victims. No intruder was safe in Vallet. And apart from Father Magloire, no white could enter without permission. This rule was sacred. Those who crossed the mulatto's path bowed low, out of fear no doubt, but mostly out of respect.

O'Dingue was as tall as Hubert, with a fine Arab head, as if his Caribbean blood originated from Maghreb. He inspired neither fear nor respect but terror. If Tonton-Hubé often tore strips off employees and servants, he also spoke to them kindly when pleased with their work; above all, he could listen to grievances, though it was unwise to complain without just cause. He could even be generous. O'Dingue was entirely different — quite without pity. He gave orders to Tonton-Hubé who obeyed them; but Tonton was felt to be the real power behind the throne, if not the actual master of Vallet; he was the *human* master. Anne de Lériv loved her Tonton. Her brief spells at the plantation richly made up for the renunciations compelled by boarding-school. Horse-racing relieved her irritation at having to play-act and at the same time produced a sense of fulness within her, and an obscure knowledge that she had inexhaustible resources in the depth of her heart, resources with which she could face whatever the future held, so long as she had Tonton-Hubé by her side.

One day during the summer holidays she came face to face with a pale rider as tall as O'Dingue, but quite bent with age. He tried to come alongside her, wanting she thought to throw her from her horse. Scarcely had she realized the danger when Tonton-Hubé galloped up and the madman, for that is what he was, slunk away.

'You're sure to see him again,' Tonton told her, 'but don't be afraid, your horse is faster than his. Just gallop towards the lake; he'll never follow you that far, the blue flame-tree blinds him. And after all, he's only a poor Béké with no teeth!

At which they burst into laughter.

They always regarded each other with frank, excited complicity. Then, as if nothing had happened, the mulatto would spur his horse and vanish towards the cane-fields.

When she told her mother of the incident, Marie de Lériv said: 'From now on, don't go riding without a switch. Above all, ask Tonton-Hubé to teach you his special "lunge".'

And the amazing musician, perhaps a little mad herself, laughed until there were tears in her eyes, and something in her voice broke.

Anne learned to use a long switch like a violin bow, and by following a series of parries, to 'place' the 'lunge'. In her exercises she nearly blinded several servants who acted as guinea-pigs. Her brothers tolerated her caprices for a while, then sent her to the devil when she became too dangerous. When she was sure of herself, she spent much of the holidays searching out the blond madman, the 'blond O'Dingue' as she would laughingly call him, without ever meeting him. When, rarely, she spotted him far off, it was he who fled in terror, spurring his horse. If she caught up with him, he sought refuge in the woods of Durivage where she didn't dare follow. Tonton had expressly forbidden her to stray in that direction. The day he gave her this warning, the smiling mulatto caressed her jaw with his warm, massive hands. She grasped his meaning and shuddered: if she disobeyed, she herself would not escape, one of *her* teeth would be cruelly drawn.

She grew up quickly, proud, supple and impetuous. She was afraid of nothing, but she looked as though butter wouldn't melt in her mouth, and fooled everyone except her favourite Tonton, who contemplated her with a smile. He had created her: neither white, nor mulatto nor black. No mameluke either, but tough, like her mother.

Marie de Lériv lived almost entirely at Vallet, but O'Dingue took her out. He took her on sailing trips round the Caribbean, that sea which at all times and in all weathers throws the islands into relief, as if enriching and consecrating them. He headed for Dominica, close by Guadeloupe, before setting his course for Martinique, Barbados, Grenada, the Windward Islands and even San Domingo, where he made solid friendships.

Nothing but horizons! Here, the cliff-face of an island rises abruptly from the sea, as if to steal gold flowers from the sun; there, a long greeny glitter visible against the blue disappears, insubstantial as a ghost. There are white isles like clouds; getting closer, they assume a purple border, and nearer still they rise out of the heat haze, then vanish just as suddenly in mist. There in the distance are strangely jagged highlands, emerald in colour from base to peak, sides ribbed with pink, yellow or violet lava. The long flat islands with no visible volcanic shape are masses of coral edged with beaches like white ribbons. Here is a steeply rising island like a vast cathedral, whose spires are mountain-tops that fold away in pleats of green, blue and grey; behind the green summits are blue ones, and behind them, jagged grey peaks that tower against the sky. One island, even seen from a great distance, cannot deceive. To start with it looks like a dark mass, a sheet of paper vigorously scrumpled up and thrown on to a billiard-table. Then, that same chaotic crystallization decks itself out in gleams of beryl shimmering to amethyst, its highest peak always hooded by a cloud. The nearer you come, its colour and the sky's seem to fall in love and feed on one another. This is the island of Martinique, and the peak which is always hooded is Pelée. The mountain around that terrible volcano is green! Deceptively peaceful, long trails of purple mingle with the sharply defined luminosity of the leaves. No matter, it is a green mountain.

They had adventures in the ports. O'Dingue and Marie strolled up and down the streets and avenues, went into brothels and frequented all the rowdy hangouts where the negroes sing, drink and dance in all simplicity, expressing the state of their souls by using their own language absolutely freely. He also introduced her into what is called 'society', pretentious, old-fashioned, and still a strong influence in colonial life. There was nowhere this middle-aged black didn't take his young woman. Neither of them paid the slightest attention to the scandal they caused. Marie even seemed to enjoy it, swept up in a fever of provocation. In any case, interest in her musical talent outweighed the problems caused by her free behaviour.

At this time, life in the tropics was sumptuous and easy, as it has perhaps always been for some. Families seized any opportunity to entertain — marriages, baptisms, birthdays, parish and official feast-days — and didn't hesitate to organize riding parties through the plains and forests, excursions in the mountains, beach and riverside picnics and boating expeditions to the little isles and dependencies, as well as to those farther away. Sometimes they spent several days visiting foreign friends, especially the Anglo-Saxons whose women were not so oppressed by ridiculous convention, and benefited from efforts to keep up with the social conditions of the mother country, where customs were more liberal than those of the French Antilles. Things moved slowly in the old colonies. They had fun of course, but the major changes brought about by the abolition of slavery were still not perceptible, and the Creole woman, while more emancipated than in the previous century, still had to brave public opinion if her separate existence was to be recognized at all. With O'Dingue behind her, Marie assaulted the conventional framework. Never was there a happier woman, all the more so because her beauty and talent earned her considerable prestige.

She was tall and elegant, with a firm, beautifully curved body that was constantly carried forwards as if by a sea-swell, with a hint of a languorous lilt, while her quivering breasts seemed to ride the surface of the water. Her abundant hair, Venetian blond, betrayed nothing of her Breton ancestor with his flaming mane, but people still wondered at the shining jet black eyes set in such a pink face. (Her daughter's eyes were sea-green.) She had fine tapering hands with skilful fingers. The lines on her hands were like the veining in marble, and where they crossed, several little stars appeared in the sign of Venus; artist's hands that loved beauty and well-being without refusing risks; perhaps she had 'psychic' hands, of the very rare Sun-Venus type.

It is too soon to tell all her adventures. Graciously tall and aristocratic in bearing — the hallmarks of her race — she made an entrance into society salons and cast an unprecedented spell on them. At times, she was frankly provocative — so long as O'Dingue was standing behind her. With an unfailing instinct, both of them went straight up to those who had strained to disguise their astonishment on seeing them arrive. What could be more outrageous than a white on the arm of a negro? Something so unusual caused a shock, which was soon followed by disapproval. Those rash enough to express it, however, were soon frozen by the audacious, sharp looks the couple directed at them. Words stuck in their throats. They enjoyed conflict more than courtesy; they came as troublemakers rather than as peaceful guests. They showed off so much that they were always at the centre of some incident or

other, and were at their most insufferable among the aristocracy.
Pushing effrontery to its limits, they breezed arm in arm into every
church they came across. The entry of this living amalgam into
such peaceful and ordered places, whites on one side, blacks on the
other, and to hell with the mulattos who were out on the square, if
anywhere, never failed to astound the regular churchgoers, not to
mention the priest himself who would interrupt the service for
several seconds, trying to understand the meaning of the intrusion.
Without taking a bit of notice of the stir they made, the couple
established themselves in a corner; O'Dingue standing, lifting his
eyes to watch the play of light through the shutters or windows;
Marie, kneeling on a priedieu, raising her pretty face towards the
big negro as if in adoration, or to grasp the meaning of his
embittered mimicry and his deeper intentions. Sometimes, quite
without warning, she rose swiftly and started up on the
harmonium. Then, the whole congregation demanded mass after
mass, and the good curé was only too delighted to multiply
absolutions and communions.

Most people were on their side and treated them like friends.
The mulattos and the negroes spared no expense to entertain
them. They were endlessly fêted, especially Marie. Her music
seemed to purify everyone, and every coloured family praised her
talent. Far from resting on her laurels, she demonstrated her gift
before poorer people in all modesty, reserving her contempt for the
rich bourgeois and the aristocrats. When invited to play violin or
piano she performed with grace, and without having to be asked a
second time, getting more and more passionately carried away.
Never had there been so many concerts for the people, such
enthusiasm, so much sunshine on the island. She was one who
adds pleasure to living.

During the terrible cyclone of 1891 which devastated
Martinique, Marie de Lériv was with O'Dingue at Morne-Rouge,
a beautiful town not far from Saint-Pierre and very close to the
Pelée crater. She went on with her concert. There were twenty-one
deaths and many casualties; but if she hadn't been there,
preventing a general panic, the disaster might have been much
worse.

From Fort-de-France to Saint-Pierre the devastation was
appalling. The cyclone blew the roofs off houses, turned others

upside down, and twisted and pulverized the covered market — an all-steel construction — crushing the terrified inhabitants who had sheltered inside it. The main ward of the military hospital, forty metres in length, an immense building for the times, collapsed on its occupants. The savannah was devastated; desolation was everywhere. Saint-Pierre harbour which had been giving shelter to about fifteen ships when the tempest was unleashed was literally swept out; four hours later every ship had been flung against the coast or carried further out to sea and sunk. In the days following the storm the sea threw up the bodies of the wretched sailors who had been on board, along with every sort of wreckage.

The death-toll for the whole island exceeded three hundred, and the number of wounded was still greater. Marie was everywhere, tending the wounded with her own hands, giving recitals to comfort the weeping families, and raising large sums of money to help those who had lost their homes.

Once the Caribbean journey was over, O'Dingue brought her home to Vallet.

The Indian welcomed them with open arms. What concern she showed for them! Her welcome was all the more moving since the wait had been an anxious one. She lavished such goodness on Marie and O'Dingue that they forgot their resentment of malicious gossip, the dangers overcome, the tiredness brought on by long-distance journeys. There is no explanation for the limitless devotion of a generous soul. Their happiness was her own, and jealousy, that cruel alternative, never raised its head. No one understood as she did the chastity and propriety of their relationship. She was full of self-sacrifice, inventive in devotion, loving and caring, courageous and of millenarian faith. She was an Indian, a Capesterre Hindu. And as time went on, her proven largeness of soul was manifested more and more.

THE ELDEST son of O'Dingue and the incomparable Indian, Baindingue-le-Câpre, came home from Paris as a Doctor of Law and laureate in the colonial magistrature examination. He married Marie's daughter, Anne the chabine, the beautiful and fascinating Creole with red hair and green eyes that were deep set to veil their mysteries.

The country was in a gala mood that day, since it was the first official marriage between a black and a white; even though Anne was a redhead, she couldn't be considered anything other than the Countess de Lériv's daughter.

At the birth of Choutoumounou and Pampou, twins as black as ebony, Vallet was filled with consternation. A mulatto was expected but two little negroes appeared, black as devils. Servants and close friends exchanged knowing glances.

O'Dingue was the great-grandson of the Big Twins, and grandfather to these 'Little Twins'. Despite his age and colour, had he then been Marie's lover when she came home from the city, a sensitive and bewildered little thing, the victim of incurable convention and a thousand different constraints? When she found herself so summarily provided with a fiancé she didn't even know, with no means of appeal against all the arrangements made over her head except in the extravagant gesture of refusal that forged her destiny? According to this hypothesis, Anne de Lériv and Baindingue had the same father — hence the blackness of their twins.

It might also be Tonton-Hubé, O'Dingue's junior and something of a sorcerer, who won the young artist. An original and mysterious figure, with red eyes that no one dared meet, guessing the intentions of men and the feelings of women, inevitable and omnipresent as the sky is overhead, warrior-like in cruelty but tempered by certain streaks of kindness — perhaps he had offered the young Creole seeking to escape the crushing monotony of a hopeless, purposeless life, the chance of unheard of novelty.

Was it he then who charmed the cloistered girl and 'unleashed' her on the brothels of Pointe-à-Pitre or Sainte-Anne, content to have her followed or chauffeured by a deaf-mute negro, O'Balou the Master of Forges? And did he not, as was his tactic, intervene at just the right moment, and then teach his conquest how to protect herself with her secret 'lunge'?

According to this hypothesis, Anne de Lériv and Baindingue were of one blood; she was thus a chabine, a little lighter than the mulatto with his bloodshot eyes. This would explain the colour of the twins, and the several other signs of a forbidden union.

But how does that explain the fact that Tonton-Hubé took her to O'Dingue, for the latter was apparently amazed to see his half-brother carrying the beautiful girl in his arms. Tonton more or less offered her up to him, and O'Dingue then bagged her for himself, while the mulatto took on his rôle as bodyguard. It was as though he 'surrendered' her to his elder, the authentic descendant of the O'O — whereas he himself had only entered the family by the back door — and could thus do no other than bring the master the 'harvest' of his lands. It's also possible that Tonton-Hubé was fully aware of how others thought, and decided to cede her to his half-brother's lightning passion, all the more so because Marie de Lériv herself seemed in awe of this extraordinary negro — not forgetting the dictum which says that she who tastes mulatto soon wants the negro.

How did the Indian like this arrangement? In the islands many women had adapted to the caprices of their husbands, and the most complex situations had been resolved by admiring a prowess honourable to the whole family. The liaison between an ageing negro and a young white, a noble to boot, might surprise and bring an involuntary smile to the lips — but one tinged with admiration.

All these hypotheses may well be pure fabrication, absurd fantasy. Marie might simply have been the lover of some wild young Béké who was then killed in a duel. In her distress she found providential refuge in an honourable family which welcomed and soon came to idolize her.

At Vallet she basked in the affection and authentic admiration her protectors had for her art; all the black workers went into ecstasies at her slightest improvisation. Vallet nurtured her dream, a dream never clearly expressed, and one which the artist seemed now to have realized. She felt at home there and had no desire to live anywhere else.

At the death of her father, Count de Lériv, she inherited Durivage; but she expressed no desire to live there, and even forbade Tonton-Hubé to cultivate it.

'Let them plant bottles and water them!' she said to the mulatto when he showed interest.

So Durivage was overrun by brushwood and bramble. No one could look at the place without recalling the great Homecoming Ball, and the feast that lit up a whole night, one long and beautiful tropical night. Nor could they contemplate without sadness what the property had become; a wasteland where few dared set foot, said to be haunted by a phantom horseman.

If Durivage, the Béké's dwelling, went to ruin, Vallet grew ever more prosperous and impressive.

Despite the stories, it is still hard to believe that the Creole sonata, the Caribbean concerto for violin and piano, the Bamboula in G minor, and the Caribbean rhapsody were all composed in that house. They were works still unknown in Europe, but they charmed generations in the Antilles. It is hard to believe that Vallet sheltered a brigand, his Indian wife and his white mistress, all guarded by a mulatto who kept unceasing vigil on the comings and goings of a crazed white who would canter endlessly round the plantation, seeking an opening through which he might avenge an inexpiable offence.

During her lifetime, Marie de Lériv had only one real ambition: to replace the wooden soundpost of her Stradivarius with a crystal one.

Even when he was very old, O'Dingue still tried, with his skilful fingers, to fulfil her dream. From every salon he surreptitiously carried away the glasses of Bohemian crystal. Back at Vallet, the poor man vainly tried to cut the little transparent cylinders to the exact size and fit them into the heart of the instrument.

Marie de Lériv died prematurely, at the start of the Great War, having only just reached her fiftieth year. Never perhaps had the sun shone down on such passions as had stirred in her. Placed on her bed facing the sea, she smiled at the Little Twins and held out her violin murmuring: 'There is a soul of crystal inside!'

Then she lay back and died. Choutoumounou and Pampou crossed themselves.

Following tradition, her body was embalmed in acacia leaves, laid in a mahogany coffin and borne off to Calvary Hill,[1] in the Grands-Fonds where her grave was prepared.

'Farewell, my soul,' murmured O'Dingue as he threw a handful of petals from the blue flame-tree on to her coffin. There are many still alive today who will tell you that the O'O wept that day, and searcely survived it. Among the witnesses is Tonton-Hubé who could tell many stories that may be no more than legends; but now he only talks to Anne de Lériv when she goes to see him in his hut, the 'bamboo cabin'. Like a good dog he remains out there, close by the tomb of Marie de Lériv, as if to guard her against the terrible ghost that continues its unbridled gallop through Durivage.

[1] The highest hill on Grande-Terre (108 m.).

WHILE still young, Choutoumounou and Pampou learned the art of boarding.

When a ship heaves into the roads, the little Antilleans sound the alarm, slip rapidly into the sea, swim out and from a distance observe the manoeuvres of their 'enemy'.

Don't for a moment think that these little devils go in search of gold or silver coins. They are much too proud, and the game they play is based on something more noble than simple greed.

In the green water, they wait patiently for a boat carrying notables to put out from the side of the ship. In triangular formation, they hold the sharks in due respect. Their small supple bodies, the colour of antique bronze, melt into the emerald mass; variegated fish worry their feet. Squalls come and go at a safe distance, never troubling the swimmers, and the trade wind ruffles their curly hair. Breathing turns to panting, and each exchanges a glance with his neighbour.

The manoeuvres are over. The anchor drops and passengers take their place in a small rowing-boat that heads straight for the landing-stage. The complicit sea goes darker, like purple ink. Little waves slap and caress the faces of the children, going glugluglug in their ears.

They glance at each other a last time, and note the position of the Boarding-Leader who usually spearheads the operation. The boat's oars dip in and out to their own slow rhythm. Then a cry, a signal:

'O'O!...'

And in the twinkling of an eye the frail skiff is overturned: for the 'Commando'[1], it's *sauve qui peut!*

On solid ground the spectators roar with laughter, especially when an official personage is thus baptized. This is what is known as boarding.

---

[1] A word of Portuguese origin, very well known in the Antilles since the sixteenth century.

One of the most famous boardings was perpetrated against Professor Jean Gostze of the Faculty of Law in Paris, who came to Guadeloupe to run as Deputy. Never had he received so hearty a welcome.

He was a combative man, with sharp eyes and a pointed beard like that of an extravagant Russian revolutionary. Baindingue, who had attended his lectures on Public Law, recounted how one day the famous professor, carried away by his own eloquence, allowed this to slip out:

'Gentlemen, royalty is dead!'

The audience began to murmur, while the followers of Maurras and other militant royalists were rallying.

With the same *élan*, the professor declared:

'And all your murmurings won't raise it up again!'

Which caused a real hullaballoo.

Baindingue, little inclined to indiscipline, deplored the bad manners of his fellow students.

Once his studies were over and he had been appointed magistrate at Pointe-à-Pitre, Baindingue kept in close touch with his former teacher. He even wanted to marry his daughter Claire, but O'Dingue opposed the idea. Baindingue assured Gostze that he would be elected in the first round because he himself would present him to the Guadeloupi people. At this period, even the dead were voters.

Once announced, the arrival of a 'Big-White' brought the playful little world of the good town Pointe-à-Pitre together. The Saintannais came to the rescue.

The Atlantic liner dropped anchor out to sea, and the professor and his daughter took their places in a rowing-boat. Claire looked about thirty, her lovely face smiled into the spray, a gentle, dreamy expression; her gaze and the curve of her lips were imbued with a subtle tenderness.

Chin level with the water, Choutoumounou watched the light play over that perfect countenance. The perpendicular noonday rays modelled her into the image of Venus. For the little negro it was love at first sight: his only thought was to take possession of that woman. And how can a negro possess the woman of his dreams if he doesn't first capture her? Before his comrades reached his side, he leapt out of the water, capsized the boat and dived back into the sea, holding his goddess in his arms. As she struggled against her ravisher, he held her all the closer. As he plunged through wave after wave, turning and turning, he entered seventh heaven, especially as the creature didn't let go of him and they became so entangled that they nearly sank straight to the bottom of the Caribbean sea. Luckily, Pampou had been following on behind and tore the hysterical siren out of his brother's arms. A moment later, on the lapis lazuli waves, a fair head held up by two little negroes threw out a kind of light far above the swell. With the help of the oarsmen everyone soon regained their places in the boat, in addition to two new passengers whom the worthy professor, soaked to the bone, held firmly. But what did that matter to Choutoumounou? For the first time in his life he had kissed a woman — and some woman! A real white! One day, he would match his ancestors, exploit for exploit.

Jean Gostze was furious when he learned who the two demons were that had capsized his boat, in the grand tradition of 'Washing the Whites' who land on the island for the first time. To come to this country at the far end of the world and to be flung into the water for your pains by your host's children, is beyond bearing. Never had he witnessed such unseemly behaviour. Could the negroes of the Antilles not control themselves and behave in a civilized fashion? They really are savages, then! The professor demanded that Choutoumounou and Pampou be punished in public, in front of his daughter and himself.

The Little Twins took the flogging they received from one of Baindingue's servants without a whimper. During their 'correction', which recalled the way the whites chastised their slaves, Chou contemplated Mademoiselle Claire, who for her part took much pleasure in noting the unfeelingness of the little monsters, even though Pampou fainted.

Chou reproached himself; too intent upon the woman, he didn't see his twin collapse, but was as though immersed in a light that flared up from the blue flame-tree under which these events occurred. All the protagonists saw the flare; reason can reason, but cannot explain it away. The link between blue flowers and sky drew out its luminous intensity in such a way that the sky darkened against the flash in a mysterious vibration. Only the young boy knew what that meant, and bellowed:

'O'O!'

It was not a whimper, not an ordinary cry, but a terrible appeal.

Tonton-Hubé appeared. He too, but from a great distance down in the cane-fields, had seen the radiant alert and was on his way, gathering helpers as he went, as though he were on the spot before the event took place. Despite his age, he seized the servant with the whip by the scruff of his neck and sent him rolling at the feet of Baindingue. He fixed his flaming red eyes on the latter, until Baindingue was forced to look away. The magistrate collapsed without having been so much as touched. Professor Gostze retired into himself, confused and ashamed. Claire, who was quite bewitched, contemplated Chou with his bleeding back, just as he brooded over her with an inexpressible tenderness.

Despite the goodwill and energy expended by Baindingue, more affable than ever towards his guests, the professor was eliminated in the first electoral round. When he rose to address the public, having been fulsomely introduced by his 'agent', two dreadful little voices chirped up:

'Goatee! . . . Goatee! . . .'

And the whole audience, suddenly aware of the honourable candidate's little pointed beard, took up the rhythm:

'Goatee, Goatee! Goatee, Goatee! Goatee, Goatee! Goat-Goatee!'

It was a catchy rhythm, suggested by Tonton-Hubé to sink the candidate. Anne supported this faction, since she soon realized that her husband was having an affair with Claire. Like any outraged Creole, her wounded egotism exacted vengeance. If Baindingue chased a negress it was not important; but to betray her with a white was too much. They flogged her children; they made off with her husband — that was how those people behaved towards the negroes! By O'O, they don't get away with that!

So Jean Gostze and his daughter had to leave Guadeloupe bowed with disappointment. Swearing a little late in the day never to trust negroes again.

The electoral campaign that began with a fine boarding ended in spectacular failure.

Since the invention of motor-boats, and the construction of quays at Pointe-à-Pitre, such boardings have become rare. Today the word boarding has another meaning: the operation is carried out by separating a dancing couple and carrying off the lady or by accosting a woman in the street. Authentic traditions will forever be prostituted . . .

Choutoumounou, the Holô King, made his conquests out at sea, and dived down to alarming depths to snatch one glorious kiss. Most of the others, though they were older, would never have dared carry a European off like that; and he was completely mad to demand no more than a kiss.

He was not just a lout up to boarding stunts; the truth was simpler, he had O'O blood in his veins. Worse, it was O'O Brittany-style, the Black and the Red Corsairs inhabited him. This was clear to the people of Sainte-Anne and Pointe-à-Pitre alike. No one looked for a confrontation with him; they cleared out double quick instead. He could put people on their guard with a single glance.

He was black as ebony, an ebony that could absorb all the sun's rays and rediffuse them, drop by drop, through the close-knit mail of his skin while retaining their essence, which was energy to burn. His delicate features contrasted with his thick lips and flat nose; they expressed a certain generosity, accentuated by a more or less permanent smile that played around the corners of his sensual mouth. It was a very ironic smile, mocking and disarming; the face would relax and the almond eyes that were dark and liquid remained active, luminous, alive, expressive, a mirror of malign joy. Then, quite suddenly, they would focus and transcend any human expression to reveal their green.

A quick glance at his face gave the impression of 'a good sort'. The first sense of unease came on meeting his gaze. His hair complicated this double impression: it was thick, dense, woolly and quite without lustre, sprouting like a wild tuft and often endearingly tousled — though that meant nothing.

A closer inspection was still more disconcerting. He seemed to be permanently quivering, his skin animated by brief shivers, like a cat's fur which puckers at the sting of an insect and goes on trembling in tensed expectation of a second contact, watching for it, not getting angry at first but soon showing signs of irritation and growling, if not actually striking out.

The moment anybody stared at him with any insistence he was on his guard. The tic in his skin became more marked. His expression hardened, becoming more terrible in proportion to the interior effort he made to control himself, waiting to strike. When he gathered himself in this way, images of battle, of heroic struggle, of strange cries and crazed hallucinations would flood his mind. When he laughed, long, sharp and slightly separated canines appeared, exultantly white.

Some element in his spirit drove him to defy everything, or else his eyes would stare into the middle distance and the universe would become empty. People would have preferred him to say something, would even speak to him to elicit some reply: nothing.

He was animated by the spirit of the Big Twins, and though still young, it wasn't only for amusement that he would hurl a row of tourists — high-ranking officials or merely passing tradesmen — overboard. He knew hatred; it was in his skin — too much so. It enters the bloodstream and regulates the rhythm of the heart; it is breathed in and exhaled as flames; the breath gets faster still, fanning the forge; there is nervous quivering in the skin; it rises to the head and oozes into the eyes; then the desire overflows, the desire to take hold of anyone, so long as it's a white, and strike and strike, break and break, tear, crush, kill, kill, kill. It is a sickness. It is hatred. Even in the sea Choutoumounou simmered. And then an inner force of undefined beneficence mastered him and made him want to break down and cry.

There was his brother Pampou as well. He was just the same, but he never cried. Together, they posed serious problems. Usually, they fled into the woods to escape deserved punishment. But there was more to their flight than the reflex of a child who wants to avoid a beating. A deep instinctive reaction was at the bottom of it, driving them on with the most varied sounds blaring in their ears: yelpings, tom-toms, cries, shrieks, bells. They would forge ahead, smashing everything on the way, and reach the edge of the wood, exhausted but radiant.

Anne de Lériv often contemplated her twins for long moments, until something melted in her breast. Having married a black, she had secretly hoped for mulattos, like Tonton-Hubé. But there they were, two black monsters.

The Little Twins, as they soon became known throughout the country, had apparently indelible African blood in their veins. Cross the Bourbons with the Austrians: you get Bourbons. A negro, who is tropicalized in the Caribbean, plunged into Eastern incense and married to a Breton girl, will still have black children. In the Baindingue family at least, Mendel's Law is not so infallible as one might expect. Chou and Pampou were Guadeloupi: Antillean. But only their mother could understand what that meant. Yes, she was proud, very proud to be the wife of a wealthy black aristocrat who owned the finest plantation on the island and who was a famous magistrate to boot; yes, she was proud to be married to a negro! But how happy she would have been had her children been mulatto . . . She loved them all the same, even too much, with a soft spot for Chou.

Chou was her *own* Big Twin. The veritable symphony of black that played over his body was a delight to behold. Besides, there was his liquid eye, his tender smile and the graceful way he held himself. But when he was ill, or gnawed by some sadness, his skin looked dirty, giving his body a gross and terrible aspect, so that he resembled Pampou; Anne found that insufferable.

What she felt looking at Chou bewildered her. He was her son, but she thought of him as a lover. A terrible thought indeed, but one which she didn't reject simply because it *was* unthinkable. It helps to explain why her sons were so attached to her.

Tall and svelte, Choutoumounou charmed her romantic Creole imagination with his small round buttocks squeezed into a pair of tight-fitting breeches that left his spindly legs bare. These breeches — and Pampou wore an identical pair — had an unusual history. They were of supple, uncreased leather, made to stand the test of time and splendidly adapted to the curves of their legs. Thrown into relief by their ebony skin, they took on an extraordinary colour. As a young girl, Anne de Lériv had worn these breeches which she had dug out of a steel-banded trunk in the corner of an attic at Vallet. But when her nanny told her the O'O had fashioned them out of 'whiteskin' she decided never to wear them again, even for riding. She questioned Tonton-Hubé, who replied with a laugh which made her shiver, that old negresses often took traditional legend for gospel truth. Despite this, every time she saw a pair of Corsair breeches she saw slavers, boardings, savage killings, dismemberings and tannery work enough to make her hide her face in horror; like her sons, she often suffered from sudden, unexplained hallucinations, triggered by the simplest of objects. But she would

reason with herself and turn admiringly to the flesh of her flesh, her
Big Twin, whose muscular torso and wide shoulders swelled out
from a narrow waist; was he not the handsomest black-mulatto in
all Guadeloupe? He could be a 'sacatra', a type of negro that
resembles the Hindu; and why not, since his grandmother was an
Indian.

The physiological and morphological features of Choutoumounou and Pampou were identical. Those closest to them could
sometimes observe differences in bearing and behaviour.
Choutoumounou's supple movements and his ability to remain
calm when faced with the unexpected, and the extreme elegance of
his speech, sewn with words beyond his years, contrasted with
Pampou's brutal and crude pugnacity. Pampou also had deep
knowledge of the vast repertory of Antillean slang, borrowed by
sailors the world over; words mixed with the sulphurous filth of a
molten volcano they are so hurtful and hateful to the ear, defiling
the insulter as much as the insulted. By their sordid or erotic
suggestiveness, they provoke a response in the same vein or worse,
leading to the inevitable struggle. But on the physical level, it was
impossible to tell the twins apart, and when they indulged in their
favourite game of imitating each other, people became exasperated
trying to identify them.

At school, Choutoumounou did all the written work while
Pampou went up to the blackboard when either of them was called.
None of the masters noticed. Baindingue got wind of their game,
and the Little Twins were placed in different schools, one in the
lycée and the other in a private school run by religious instructors.
This arrangement changed nothing; it was easy for the pupils to
play tricks on those honourable institutions. In exasperation,
Baindingue had Pampou's forehead branded, and pointed this out
to the different teachers and directors of the two schools. A few
days later, Choutoumounou appeared with the same distinguishing mark on his forehead before Brother Elyjius in the famous
private college in Pointe-à-Pitre, while Pampou, with a smile all
over his face, underwent the close scrutiny of the senior master at
the Lycée Carnot.

Baindingue and his wife Anne could instantly distinguish their
impossible offspring. There was no question of duping them, and
Choutoumounou had no intention of trying to do so; he was who he

was, and proud of it.

His father used this occasion to make his point. With the insinuating manner of a magistrate addressing a suspect he asked him:

'And who branded you?'

Chou looked him in the eye for a while, as if to get rid of some misunderstanding, and then, quite suddenly:

'Who branded *me*? . . . Ah! And who branded Pampou?'

Astonished as he was, Baindingue should have bided his time; but he exploded with fury:

'Shameless little devil! So now *you're* asking the questions!'

'. . .'

Choutoumounou remained coldly controlled.

He could always keep silent when he chose to, and nothing could breach that silence except what preoccupied him at the time: his attention was fixed more on what he was ruminating than on what was said to him.

'Well, are you going to answer me?' Baindingue demanded.

Nothing his father said stirred Chou, who was waiting for the first insult and the threats.

'Do you want a flogging?'

Then the boy spat out his cutting answer:

'O'O was flogged — but by the Old-Whites!'

For a mere boy to bring up the horrors of the recent past bordered on insult. Baindingue was being called a slave trader unambiguously by his own son.

The magistrate managed to swallow his shame and embarrassment, and in a moment of intense thought decided: he would consult Monsignor Magloire, the family confessor. O'Balou's old friend, now a prelate, had lost something of his sixth sense; he advised separating the brothers completely until they were more malleable.

Pampou was to be sent to school with the Brothers, and the prelate took it upon himself to recommend the boy to Brother Elyjius whose task it would be to educate him.

The twins deserved flogging more frequently than they got it. However much one loves one's children and is concerned for their future, it is impossible to help them without renouncing sentimentality. The only way is to tame them, without worrying too much about the marks inflicted on their bodies: character must be built willy-nilly. And Brother Elyjius, a holy man, knew how to do it.

Choutoumounou was to be prepared for the classical disciplines. An intelligent boy, he could go far, but he too had to be brought to heel. Life at the *lycée*, or in a private college, seemed a bit soft for a tough young man like him. Send him out into the world! It would have been best to despatch him straight to Paris, but he was still too young. For the present, they decided, the thing to do was to set him and his tutor afloat on the schooner of his uncle, the famous captain who practised coastal trading in memory of O'O the Corsair. The boy would learn to bow before such a man. Also, contact with the fabulous mixed population of the Caribbean, seen in its full variety, and practice in speaking Creole dialects, French, English and other languages, would help build up his character and bring it to maturity. Studying people and learning their tongues are two profitable sources of knowledge. Above all, it was necessary to tear the boy away from his brother and save him. More than one difficult son has had to fall in with his father's wishes, and has lived to thank him afterwards.

Such was the advice of Monsignor Magloire.

Anne de Lériv set herself against sending Chou on his uncle's schooner. She knew the man's brutality. But she protested in vain. She tried to soften her husband's resolve by putting a heart-rending inflexion into her cooing voice and watering her arguments with tears. Baindingue held firmly to his decision. The master had spoken, and there was nothing more to be said. The Little Twins would be brought to heel, that was all there was to it.

If someone had told Baindingue he would live to regret his decision, he would have shrugged. Great jurist that he was, he had yet to discover the effect constraint can have on the soul of a child.

Anne de Lériv had never before had a serious disagreement with her husband. She still loved him, though of late she had fallen to dreaming of the time when he was only her fiancé and had to fulfil her every whim. Since his return from Paris and their marriage, he had behaved odiously, treating her exactly as the whites treated their women: as favourite slaves, loved and flattered to be sure, but slaves all the same. Like them too, he was unfaithful, going with servant girls and maids, even with white women visiting the colonies, profiting from each opportunity as it arose, creating opportunities by inviting friends from France to spend their holidays on the beautiful ancestral property: Vallet-les-Bains! Since the war was raging in Europe, he abstained from inviting his Parisian friends.

If Tonton-Hubé hadn't stopped him, he would have done up Durivage — her own property — and turned it into some kind of warehouse!

'I hope he doesn't think I shall always be so submissive,' she thought furiously to herself.

Were they perhaps trying to call her to order as well? She had studied Baindingue over the years. His brilliant career as a magistrate intoxicated him with glory; for a complete negro, he acted too much the Big White. So it was.

Deprived of her children, especially Chou, she was deeply affected. She took comfort, as usual, in Tonton-Hubé.

'You can be sure,' the indestructible old magician told her, 'we shall see those two again before two cyclones are out!'

And the weird mulatto smiled. She understood what he meant and waited patiently.

On the day of their separation, Pampou leaving for Pointe-à-Pitre as a boarder, and Choutoumounou marched off by a mentor to his uncle's schooner, Anne de Lériv cried a little all the same, as if she foresaw some catastrophe.

Seeing their mother's tears, the Little Twins looked at each other for support in their despair.

It was during a maths lesson that Pampou decided to become a runaway negro.

Before embarking on Pythagoras's theorem, Brother Elyjius had thought it fitting to fix the attention of his pupils by starting with a brief historical reminder of the life in Greece about five hundred years before Jesus Christ. He noted with humour that the island of Samos was less glorious for the scent of its muscat wine than as the birthplace of the celebrated philosopher-mathematician, and that there was no sufficient or fated reason why the island of Guadeloupe should remain eternally in man's memory as the illustrious cradle of rum production.

Most of the little negroes in the class didn't understand a word Brother Elyjius was saying, but they gobbled out their laughs and chuckles like turkeys, to show they understood.

Pampou wondered what the master had said to rouse his companions, and why they were guffawing in this way. Were they by any chance laughing at him? He had no prestige in this school because he had come from the *lycée*; he didn't know their habits or way of speaking, he didn't know their games, and above all Chou wasn't with him. Getting used to a new school was a lot worse than brawling with strangers on the quayside. He would have sold his soul to the devil to cruise round the Caribbean islands like his brother — there were more fabulous discoveries to be made there than any Aegean sea could boast, including Samos which was only good for producing bizarre beings like Pythagon, Pythaqui's theorem? That school and that beak were no use to him, and what good was the 'great period' before Jesus Christ? And what did *he* have to do with it all anyway? In this stupid school they never stopped reminding you — even in the context of mathematical abstraction — that human history consisted of two chapters: one before Jesus Christ and the other after! As if there wasn't always a before and after. Surely before O'O and after O'O was all that mattered.

It wouldn't have taken much to make him say some pretty unpleasant things to this garrulous priest.

His head buzzed with all this, but he kept his peace, though not for long.

When the classroom was quiet once more, though Pampou remained on his guard, Brother Elyjius began his demonstration of the famous theorem, drawing different diagrams on the blackboard and putting one within the other, using straight and dotted lines, capital letters here, small letters there, following conventions that seemed simple enough to the teacher but perfectly unintelligible to brains more accustomed to the real trajectories followed by stones hurled into three-dimensional spaces where mangoes were ripening, than to the orthomorphic projections of a geometry damagingly reduced to the inconceivable dimensions of space in a pinpoint, connected to a vectoral space by structural induction. Pampou followed with difficulty; he was an intelligent boy and wanted to understand. Before long he noticed that the Brother used either hand with equal ease to write on the blackboard, and that both were horribly crippled. It is remarkable enough to see a teacher writing with both hands — now with the right, now with the left — for ambidextrousness is rare; but each of these hands had fingers missing, and that was enough to rouse the most basic curiosity. Brother Elyjius opened his hand in such a way as to reveal three little pink stumps at the end of his sleeve. The other was the same.

Pampou counted the fingers: three on the left hand and three on the right. A troubling sum. Then illumination came. Each hand represented a triangle, and as the fingers looked equal, they were equilateral triangles. Conclusion; two equilateral triangles make a right angle! QED! The demonstration went home almost instantaneously.

Delighted with himself, Pampou undertook a still closer scrutiny of Brother Elyjius's person and movements. On each hand, three little stumps gripped the chalk; so, two fingers were missing which, counting the other hand, made four. Four? The perfect square, since two plus two make four and two times two, mysteriously enough, make four as well. That was worth pondering. Pampou noticed the Brother's bandy legs. A steel brace appeared every now and then from beneath the torn soutane. Now, were there two hypotenuse angles within a right-angle triangle?

Brother Elyjius was of Dutch origin, very fair, with an animated face that bore the marks of nobility. In his youth he had fallen victim to polio which had left his limbs riddled with weaknesses, but his blue eyes shone with intelligence, altering in moments of action to flashes of anger; at other times, most often when he was alone, they expressed pain, as if imploring some consolation for his loss.

No one could have wished for a more devoted teacher, or one more conscious of his high educational and formative mission; he always prepared his lessons with care and put them in context by means of preliminary explanation and quotation. His faith in God sustained him in the active optimism he showed before his pupils in class and his flock at mass, when he would make rapid movements as if to cast out the devil.

Pampou was still young; he could not understand this holy man engaged in demonstrating the most famous axiom in the history of mathematics; he pursued his parallel calculation, based on a mischievous system of correspondences.

Brother Elyjius, who felt the presence of an occult force in the room, turned round and let his eyes wander from row to row, hunting out the culprit. Finally, his gaze came to rest on Pampou, lost on a projection of his own, wondering why geometrical figures did not change their shapes when turned from edge to edge, and why when one triangle was superimposed upon another its dimensions didn't modify from the very fact of it having been moved, and how could a double hypotenuse of variable angle be made to meet according to such movements — Brother Elyjius's legs going back and forth in front of the blackboard — on a perfectly defined but immaterial cross-section?

It was at this moment that the Brother burst in upon this non-Euclidean universe.

'Why are you looking at me like that?'

There was no evading this direct, unambiguous question, followed up by three crooked fingers pointed straight at the pupil.

'Me? Me, Brother?'

'Yes you, you Choutoumounou.'

The class was alerted; the Brother had made a mistake. The accused party started visibly.

'But . . . but . . . Brother, sir, I'm not looking at you . . . and I'm not, no I'm not Choutoumounou. He's my brother, and I'm Pampou, I swear it!'

'Oh prodigious,' exclaimed Brother Elyjius. 'He denies looking at me when his diabolical eyes stare insolently at me. O Lord of the Resurrection! He says he's called Pampou when everyone knows his name is Choutoumounou! Heavenly God, is it surprising that civilized people think negroes are all liars? I tremble to think of the supreme punishment which will strike this Satan-face. And don't look at me like that, you little lout!'

With his hand stretched out in front of him, Brother Elyjius came limping down from the podium, almost without movement as his twisted legs swallowed up the steps. He looked like a ghost, moving without walking. A thrill of sadistic joy went round the benches. The twisted fingers made straight for Pampou's eyes as they boggled with horror. The feverish roar of blood in the ears of the unhappy boy, combined with the fear in his head, made him unable to feel and act like the others; whenever he felt threatened, he experienced an inexplicable and desperate crisis.

In one bound he was in the middle of the room. As if through a cyclone, sprays of multi-coloured leaves, red, black and white stones torn up from the earth and men with whips restraining mastiffs on leads assailed him, as a horrible cry came from his throat:

'O'O!'

Brother Elyjius was felled, benches hurled against each other, tables smashed, doors in splinters, bits of shutter flying in the air, all in one fantastic racket.

Once outside, the boy's legs went wild. Flight!

Like an arrow, Pampou crossed the luminous banners the sun had laid over the drowsy island, as yet unaware of the drama, during its siesta. The hot, damp air enveloped the houses and lapped the streets, bringing threads of liquid silk down to the moist earth that was wrapped in tall waves of silence and the scents of storm, of bitter mildew and wild gums. He ran towards the ridge. An extended trembling started on the glassy water and a soft breeze blew in from the sea. From inlet to inlet, over black rocks covered with seaweed, he got to Gosier beach without stopping. Caught up in the speed of his flight, he would have flung himself into the water, boarded the famous neighbouring island and climbed to the top of its lighthouse to scan the horizon for the sails of Choutoumounou's boat. A brave, vain, extravagant project flashed on his mind, and he rejected it instantly, standing before the sea grown suddenly rough, as if in warning.

It was a signal he recognized, confirmed by hundreds of crabs which scuttled rapidly into gaps in the vegetation or fissures in the rock. Pampou was a child used to evil spells and he knew how to get free of them. A cyclone was in the air.

At the slightest, darkest sign, everything inside him shook with the strengths and weaknesses of youth. Changing course, he made for the great undulating plains, gold, green, sap green, a blueish metallic green, and red and yellow, crowned afar by the swarm of whiteish pennants that marked the cane-fields.

Here, the extreme heat was intoxicating. He made a wide detour through lemon and orange groves and the thick tangle of tamarind-trees. Then, following the columns of palm and coconut, running or walking past a quarry of stones that are malleable when extracted, hard as granite a few days later, he descended still lower and skirted the vast expanse of Durivage, that place his mother owned which was left in ruins because, so they said, it was haunted by his great-grandfather, Count de Lériv. Pampou passed behind the church of Sainte-Anne and headed for the sandy beach which spread to infinity like an adamantine river on one side of the calm and shallow sea. There he chose to halt. In a convulsion of nerves, the angry child flung himself on the sand.

The beach of Sainte-Anne is a flirt; she changes her dress for each lover, and decks herself out in adorable little necklaces for every pair of eyes. And yet, she's the most faithful of mistresses, and her desertions only illustrate the unfathomable mysteries of love. What would she not do to satisfy Pampou? He breaks through her languor, lifts her hair, rips off her jewels and embraces her with rage, tearing the whiteness of her skin, covering and bruising her body with his kisses like the sea on a stormy day — and yet she welcomes him with open arms. How many times before had she clasped him to her maternal breast to dry his tears; how many times had she given herself to him, in pure and generous intimacy, to appease his passions; and how many times had she offered herself, in her bed streaming with emeralds like the depths of the

sea lit up by rays of the sun, in response to his thirst for the
unknown thing which he had not yet quite formulated. So! He
would be her Pampou, and she would be his alone, if he wanted
her, since now he seemed to understand how he must take her. She
opened to him, warm and eager, with all her veils lifted, veils of
azure, pearl and opal, all scattered to the four winds. She dreamt of
love, melancholy like a great thing that has no soul.

The impetuous child seized and pressed hard against her,
gathering her up against him, fusing his black, maddened body
with the white one that welcomed him and married his every
movement. His tongue was in her salt mouth, finding a new taste,
and he lost himself between her limbs that seemed to come alive in
dust vibrant with pleasure. All his senses sought the tenderest
spots, and his eagerness became a frenzy. His muscles tensed and
he braced himself. A burning arrow set his neck on edge and
travelled down his spine to explode in a thousand maddening
shivers. Almost suffocating, he grasped her even closer to him, to
embrace her hard. Then he lost himself in a final spasm.

Singing sun! What a strange and powerful music came from
seventh heaven then, with its unnumbered stars beyond the
firmament. Through such vast disturbance, the echoes of sounds
and lights vibrate. Everywhere gold, incense, myrrh was flowering. And now, on the naked whiteness of the beach, a frightened
shadow moved.

Distraught Pampou got to his feet. He wanted more than
anything to die.

It was only a sweet little sin, the first. His sex hung limp, rubbed
by the sand. He might have felt some stirrings of self-disgust within
him but 'Sweet are the solitary/Hidden little sins!'

He scanned the horizon where the coral belt embraced the huge
green basin of water, to make quite sure his brother Choutoumounou wasn't sailing past.

At the end of the coastal peninsula with its strange forms
modelled by wind and sea, he saw the Pointe des Châteaux, an
outcrop familiar to navigators, and, further out, the little Ile de la
Désirade[1]. Nothing else. He stood on tiptoe and craned his neck as

---

[1] The Island of Desire, Christopher Columbus's first sight of land when he came
from Europe four centuries ago.

if to look over the highlands to the north, in the Atlantic. He sought, but without any chance of seeing, the wild vision he had carried in his head since early childhood: the Porte d'Enfer, whose two baroque but natural columns, as tall as royal palms, rest on the deep sea reef. They are topped by an archway where the east wind buffets and the waves break and scatter. In a capricious moment, nature had fashioned this Dantesque work in front of a deep bay. In days gone by, no one had suspected that behind the ceaseless flecks of foam the original O'O lurked in his sloop, ready to bear down on the slavers. That was where Pampou wanted to take refuge, but he saw nothing under the blazing sun except Vallet masking the horizon.

Cloaked in scarlet flame-trees, a cheerlessness brooded over the house; but all around stretched the variously golden savannah with its clumps of age-old tamarind and giant cacti, its large patches of iridescent grasses and its elegant coconut-trees with swollen fruit — like the breasts of Sainte-Anne women — and full of matchless milk. In the deepening shadow of green mango-trees, herds of black cattle stand motionless. The metallic surface of the pond is flecked by large white-hemmed leaves, soft water-lilies set off by red and yellow canna flowers, and under the strange blue flame-tree lazed every type of moorhen, duck and bunting. The scattered piping of humming-birds could be heard as the trade winds died down.

Beyond this sleepy pastoral stretches the rustling blond expanse of cane-fields. The cutters are there, hidden by the shadow of straw hats shaped like mushrooms and big as umbrellas; their tanned naked torsos stream with sweat and their backs bend towards the earth. Their breeches offer no protection against small stinging plants. Blade in hand they cut the juicy stems, while the binders follow, each woman behind her man; their backs are bent too, corsets holding in large chests, wide canvas skirts tucked and knotted between thighs and buttocks that bounce at each step. They gather, sort and bind bundle after bundle and put them in piles, gasping, wheezing, unable to go on but going on nevertheless, dragging behind their companions, following the rapid rhythm of the knife despite the implacable sun. What a wretched scene . . . The vigilant supervisor is there, cantering about on horseback to left and right. No one can rest a moment without some brutal remark and an order to jump to and get back to work.

Neighbouring all this misery is the dark, impenetrable mass of the Grands-Fonds. Trees, bushes, climbing bramble and creeper run from bole to bole like a schooner's rigging. There are oaks and tall Caribbean cedars alongside the acacias, while other dry and knotted trees writhe up like skeletons. A manchineel lets fall its bitter apples. Anyone who so much as tastes the milky sap of its fruit dies in horrible agony. It is dangerous even to sit in the shadow of that cursed tree: its foliage is poisonous. Scattered palms and coconut-trees grow to great heights in search of sunlight, for the sun gets lost in this jungle. There is perpetual moisture in the air, and the woods decay.

Pampou gazed at the scene excitedly, still looking for his ancestor's hideout.

Suddenly, he saw the blue flame-tree signal and heard a long drawn-out cry:

'O'O!'

Through the hazy blue air came a wind like silk. A purpling wave was spreading, streaked with lilac and tinged with green. It was as though, suspended in the sky, imperceptible and inorganic substances were shaking, each molecule breathing separately.

A grass-coloured cricket with ruby eyes chirped once, and then the distant call again, altering the atmosphere:

'O'O!'

As the sun beat on the sea, raising bows of coloured vapour, Pampou, who seemed borne on the vegetation and mingled with the magic waves, after his twenty-five-kilometre race from Pointe-à-Pitre and the shock of his sexual discovery on the beach, tireless Pampou was again alert. He skirted the cane-fields, crossed the plain, and reached the edge of the forest. Fearless now, he plunged right in, and took his guiltless course towards Calvary Hill.[1]

Go find him in the forest then!

[1] See footnote on p. 80.

Pointe-à-Pitre divided into two camps: those who wanted to see Pampou banished from all educational establishments, and those who found it intolerable that a teacher — and a religious one what's more — should call the negroes liars, and go so far as to try to put out the eyes of the most remarkable Antillean boy, the incomparable Pampou, as he swore he was himself and not his brother. Only priests got away with that kind of injustice. Since Father Labat's time there had been quite enough churchmen infesting the country, so why not be done with it and fling them into the sea, Monsignor Magloire and his clique along with them. As expected, the Békés and the European residents joined the first camp and the authentic Guadeloupis the second. Supporters of Magloire held a more ambiguous, if not downright hypocritical position.

Anne de Lériv was not especially fond of Pampou, but she showed a mother's concern over the disappearance of her turbulent son, while her husband, Baindingue, regretted the consequences of his educational policy. The son of a highly-placed magistrate rubbing a priest in the dust had all the makings of scandal. It was he, too, who had to order the police to hunt Pampou out. Cruel decision!

But Pampou was not to be found. There were traces of him everywhere. Some said he was hiding out with a Caribbean girl from Anse Bertrand, a seaside village to the extreme north of Grande-Terre, not far from the Porte d'Enfer, where descendants of the first inhabitants of Karukéra — Fine Water Island, or Guadeloupe — lived together in very nearly their original state. Others believed that he was living out a perfect love idyll with a mulatto girl from Saint-Claude, a little community at the foot of the Soufrière. With his companion, he would sometimes hide in the flowering gardens in that beautiful oasis, and sometimes go bathing in the springs that were full of salt and iron, where they were camouflaged by the dense screen of creeper and mango branches, bamboo and tamarind. The miraculous waters of the Yellow-Bath seemed to protect the boy.

Still others held that he frolicked on the beach of Sainte-Anne, joined by girls the colours of the sea. It is even claimed that Pampou's loves inspired the local poet to write in celebration of that beach. Whatever the truth of the matter, Pampou's adventures with the most beautiful Guadeloupi girls soon became part of Caribbean folklore. There is a song about him:

> Pampou the runaway is in the woods
> My dears, my darlings!
> Who held Pampou captive?
> Who put him on the cross?
> A lovely girl, my darlings!

All these songs are light and gay, scattered with satirical phrases. Each word has a mischievous double-meaning, and each rhyming stanza recounts mad feats of love, whether on the beaches, in the water, under cover of the undergrowth or in the middle of the cane-fields. In them, Pampou thrashes the priests, tricks the police and rapes the local girls. But the real Pampou remained nothing but himself, young and inexperienced, pursued forever by those crooked fingers in their right-angled triangle. He sought his twin brother everywhere; and at every halt on his maddened flight he tended his spirit that had been wounded by his solitary revelation.

Even Monsignor Magloire had given his soul up for lost.

THINGS were even worse for Choutoumounou.

The schooner to which his father had banished him left the Pointe-à-Pitre quayside as the first streaks of the rising sun illuminated the numerous tiny glass-green islets in the bay; they responded with the endlessly renewed grace of floating things.

The red-tiled roofs of the green and yellow houses took fire. Flowers sang in the streets, while further off the slender coconut-trees on the hills shook their manes, and the rich contours of Houëlmont came into focus. Behind it rose the Soufrière, wrapped in haze at the edge of the horizon. Nature, as she has from the legendary dawn of earth, repeated once more her great poem of lights and colours, while the scent of sugar and syrup, rising from nearby factories, attested to the presence of man.

The boat plunged out into the sea. It soon left the turbulent saline river channel behind, the liquid arm that separated the two islands that make up Guadeloupe; it slipped past the ragged cliffs of black rock, the pre-Columbian megaliths, the sand and shingle beaches, the clumps of seaweed flashing to amethyst. It set off at a lively speed, with a favourable breeze, and followed the coastline that was washed by blue and green waves crested with foam.

All morning the sea swell increased and the warm breeze blew. The sea changed colour several times. The blue expired and was replaced by indigo. Then another immaculate blue answered that of the sky. Flying fish travelled like arrows through purple sunrays and then fell back, their desire to fly towards the great airy spaces unfulfilled. Drifting aimlessly, seagulls dreamed like girls.

From a boat it seems as though the island will never disappear from sight. The peak of the volcano rises higher and higher into the sky. Soon the fort of Richepanse[1], said to contain Napoleon's treasure, heaves into view, and at last Basse-Terre, a town built like an amphitheatre round a symmetrical bay, ennobled by rounded buttresses and covered with vegetation.

[1] Originally called Fort Saint-Charles, built by Houël in 1643.

Since leaving Pointe-à-Pitre, Choutoumounou had done nothing but gaze towards the Soufrière. He gazed and said nothing. He knew well that boiling volcano. He heard Pampou in his head, talking of their mad hikes over the peaks of Saint-Claude when their parents would take them up for 'a change of air'.[1] He saw Pampou and himself listening to the foamy springs that gushed forth crystalline water, or bathing in the famous rivers that flow down to the sea: the Gommier, the Malonga, the Rivière Noire and the Rivière Saint-Louis, which unite to form that most sacred symbol, the Rivière des Pères. Further on flows the Rivière aux Ecrevisses with its giant Wassous[2] and the Rivière Rouge where fish die because the water is glacial, but tired spirits can plunge to regain faith and joy.

Chou recalled a fragment of a poem:

> Oh scented haven, enchanting mountain,
> Opalescent gem, mosaic of passion
> Where the canna's shadow broods in ancient voice! . . .

He thought he heard the ancestral call:
'O'O! . . .'
It came from a long way off. How can such loneliness be endured?

'What will they do to Pampou?' the young man suddenly asked himself.

Everything, light or shade, plain or mountain, earth or sea, brings his twin to mind. They exist as one and cannot understand their separation. He can see them both, himself calm, Pampou rash and violent; he in reflective mood, but ready to strike, Pampou already calm again; he foreseeing an obstacle, Pampou in the centre of the storm from which he must rescue him.

. . . What a preposterous idea it was, cloistering Pampou with the Brothers and putting Choutoumounou on a boat to work for his exams under a tutor! Is *that* common sense? His resourceful father had obviously gone soft in the head; even O'Dingue's grandfather wouldn't have entertained such an idea! He doesn't love me or my brother. Does he really think he can imprison me forever on this

---

[1] Creole expression for going on holiday.
[2] Creole name for a type of crayfish called 'king of the source'.

corsair, while Pampou is shut up with the priests like the Big Twins were before us?

Chou thought hard and heard nothing. He didn't even notice their arrival at Basse-Terre. The sea was calm, and there were several sailing-boats at the quayside. He gazed with unseeing eyes at the wide bay. What was the movement of barges loading and unloading the schooner, or the foul-mouthed sailors stripped to the waist — what were these things to him? He was deaf to the shouting crew and the great oafish voice of his uncle, the captain, which rose above the general tumult. This noisy activity escaped Choutoumounou: he was lost in a waking dream. He hardened his resolve. The involuntary slip he had made, calling his uncle's old tub a 'corsair', filled him with secret, exalting memories. Soon, from his thoughts' depths, a voice came to him, a beautiful voice whose purity nothing could spoil. The voice said nothing, pronounced not a single syllable, but it enthralled him to the very fibre of his being. The light and colour of the tropics, the caress of the sea-wind, the fluidity of the altering air, all, all carried him up towards a spiritual region where hope is infinite and pulsing; yet he covered his face and was convulsed by sobs torn from his tense soul by a bitter sense of solitude. Looking out to sea, Choutoumounou wept.

After a brief night stopover at Marie-Galante, scarcely visible now under the constellations massed around the Southern Cross, and an even briefer respite at Dominica, the schooner made straight for Martinique. It left a wake with fiery edges, and waves fell back in a rain of sparks that seemed to reply one last time to the winkings in the sky. Great screens of spray flared up before being swallowed up in the blackness.

Little by little the dreary greyness of the night blurred. The water turned a pale, ashen blue while the sky took on tints of green. Things were astir as wavelets lapped the hull, whispering among themselves, telling secrets. In the rigging, a loud voice punctuated the pitching of the ship:

'Whoh – oh! . . . Whoh – oh! . . . O'!'

Further off, muffled slappings and splashings echoed the sound. Then the delicately stained sea veered to a violet tint, one of its commonest shades, countered by flecks of blazing foam.

They hardly slept at all. Island to island trading in the

Caribbean is tough business. Well before dawn, Choutoumounou
was up, leaning against the rail. A desire he could not quell was
buried deep in him; had he been more like others he would have
enjoyed this voyage. But nothing was exciting without Pampou.
And then there was his tutor who wouldn't let him alone. He was in
his forties, had narrow shoulders, the nose of a ferret and an
unpleasant voice. Chou began to find him irritating.

The fresh sea air soothed him somewhat, and he decided to pay
no more attention to the man's presence. Disturbance in the sea
announced the flooding of the sky. The stars disappeared and the
wind rose, swelling the sound against the hull and in the sails. It
seemed to be made up of countless crackings and grindings,
clappings, whisperings and sighings sustained by the murmuring
heart of the breaking waves.

Choutoumounou trembled and cried with joy:

'*Mi, Kanal Dominique, mi!*' (There's the Dominica canal —
over there!)

'Please speak in French,' said his teacher, looking him up and
down with contempt.

Choutoumounou, who was bare-footed and wearing his leather
corsair breeches and an open-necked Madras shirt, shrugged his
shoulders and said to himself: 'Ciwp!'[1] an implosive word
expressing disgust, and continued to contemplate the sea as if
nothing had been said.

The tutor felt not hostility but sheer blankness in front of him.

'Choutoumounou,' he said after a few moments of reflection,
'don't be arrogant, and allow me to give you some disinterested
advice. I've examined your schoolbooks and you have the makings
of a good student if only you will get down to some work. Above all,
you must realize that Creole slang is the worst of calamities,
massacring as it does the French language which is the most
beautiful in the world. The genius of French, which is to say its
clarity, order and measure, its sheer reasonableness that leaves
nevertheless a large area for feeling and free expression, lies in its
ability to reflect the most civilized thought without distortion.
What is so curious about your pidgin is your conviction that you
speak well, and the foreigner imitates it to flatter you. You try

[1] Very roughly, Darn! or Shit! but the Creole expression is more delicate.

hard, perhaps, to imitate the European languages, but believe me, more often than not the European, the white — the Béké as you say — is inclined to consider it a linguistic phenomenon peculiar to savages, and to amuse himself at your expense! Come, come young man, you must renounce the little negro in you! Your father has charged me with shaping you, and even with your education which has been sadly neglected until now. We shall begin by learning French. From now on, indeed, I want you to speak only in French, and in good French, mind, not Creole. Declare war, if you must, on rhetoric; but live in peace with syntax, as Victor Hugo demanded. We must also speak in English, in good English. Have you noticed how pure the English is in Dominica? It isn't pidgin, but very good English, and the chaotic Creole on that island is only spoken by the lowest classes that infest the ports. Finally, to be fully cultivated it isn't enough just to know French and English; you will do well to learn Greek and Latin too, so that you can read the classics in the original and extract their essence. If you put your trust in me, I'll make an educated negro out of you!'

Choutoumounou's indifference turned to hatred. From that moment he counted the tutor his personal enemy. His hands closed over the rail until his joints cracked. To despise one of the most harmonious languages in the world as 'pidgin' was not to be borne. Creole is not, in fact, a murderous failed attempt to reproduce the French language, but the historic result of social adaptation to life in the Caribbean, created out of the chaotic meeting of nearly all the European languages over the nineteenth and twentieth centuries. Its accentual values, with strong intonations — unknown in France — that distinguish it from jargon, dialect and slang, place it among those rare means of communication that can expect to meet with almost universal understanding. From the lowest class upwards, generations of Antillean youths intensely discuss the topic. Unlike the stupidity of this 'Little White', the Old Whites, the Békés, appreciated the Creole language. Faced with this *mayngywé*, this sandfly, this mosquito, Choutoumounou did not deign so much as to turn his eyes from the horizon.

The tutor, who had felt a blankness in front of him and contentedly started to fill it, was pleased enough with his arguments and the sound of his own voice to express himself more fully.

'Choutoumounou,' he went on, 'you must replace your traditional habits of confusion, nonchalance, softness, physical and intellectual laziness, with a taste for order, movement and precision of thought which will stand you in good stead to acquire a language like French . . .' The teacher rattled on, and still Chou shut him out; his voice passed over like a wind in the rigging, although the sea-wind sings a sweet and captivating melody from which Creole borrows its languorous intonation, whereas this man cawed like a crow.

The sky lightened as the sun rose on the horizon, and the sea began to flower into blue. The ship danced on the water, responding to the waves with all its sails up, with the shrieks of its pulleys, the whistling in the rigging, the billowing canvas; and loudest, the foremast creaking in the wind.

'Whoh – oh! . . . Whoh! oh! . . . O'O! . . .'

Sailors came and went, washing down the bridge with a liberal flood of water, asking the 'missiés' to get out of the way so as not to get soaked.

Two of them overheard the tutor speaking to Chou; the young man's aloofness intrigued them enough to listen more closely to the conversation, or rather the soliloquy. They gathered that the white was criticizing their language; quite naturally they began to jabber in a wholly incomprehensible slang spiced with extravagant words.

'*Béké la ka grigné!*' (The whitey's making faces.)

'*Si mwé pa té obligé, mwé pa té ké thwavay bômaté, mè, domi pou iéwé en fancè.*' (If I didn't have to, I wouldn't go to work in the early morning but would sleep my booze off and dream in French.)

'*Gadé bagaye-la si téta Béké-là?. Çà sthwodiné!*' (Have you seen the whitey's hat? It's extraordinary!)

Choutoumounou smiled imperceptibly. He soon realized that the sailors had overheard his tutor; they had discovered that he understood Guadeloupi Creole and so expressed themselves in the Dominica version, mixed in with words from Martinique like *bagaye*, which means baggage, while the Guadeloupi would have said *bitin*, which derives from 'butin' or 'booty', and generally complicating matters by using baroque expressions like *sthwodiné* from San Domingo.

It would have been too easy had the sailors simply said: '*Gadè*

Kyap là si téta Béké-là: ouais!' — which means, word for word:
look at that hat on the whiteman's head: hey!

Determined resolutely to impose his own language, the tutor
suddenly said:

'Insolence is a failing peculiar to primitive peoples, and their
language reflects their morals. Between Guadeloupe and
Martinique is like being between Scylla and Charybdis, but thanks
to school and university education we hope to save a good many
negroes from mere chaos! Young man, you are going to undertake
a long voyage with me as your constant companion. It will be a
kind of odyssey, a journey full of adventure and movement,
because I intend to make you jump to and taste the exacting
discipline necessary to attain knowledge, and that despite your
fanciful ideas and bad manners. You are my man, and I shall make
you . . .'

Choutoumounou still pretended not to hear, and went on gazing
at the horizon.

The silhouette of Dominica cathedral grew fainter and fainter
against the indigo sea. The mountains disappeared into the clouds.
The irregularities of the coastline blurred and became indistinct.
The sea changed colour yet again and flashed with tints of
turquoise as if to find its image in the sky, crossing through vapours
that hung like diaphanous veils in space. The growing light
produced rays of purple, violet, pale blue and molten gold upon the
tide.

'*Hé-hé!*' cried the boy, suddenly talkative, '*Hé-hé! . . . Mi
"delphinus" ka vini di nou bonyou!*'

A school of dolphin, swimming in single file like warships in
action and uttering stifled cries and whistles, drew near the boat,
leaping through the dove-grey sea. They were out on a boarding
spree! Like a group of clowns they started to show off to the crew
gathered on the bridge. These innocent, intelligent mammals
always like to communicate with men. Some leapt more than two
metres above the waves, turning their heads to greet the
spectators, giving little cries and piping calls. The Antilleans, all
great gamblers, were soon laying bets. The dolphins knew what
was expected of them and fell into line, preparing to leap in turn.
One remarkable grey dolphin took the lead, but the others
followed on so fast it became impossible to distinguish between

them. They came back once more, and their grey leader leapt joyfully out of the water, turned and fell straight back without a splash: she knew she had won. The sailors shouted, contesting the result of the second round since the troupe had decided to surround the boat. The grey one swam right under the hull and came back for a second leap, speaking in strange cries and standing upright on a tail that fanned the water, moving backwards and performing graceful parabolas to proclaim her victory.

Then, a quick dry shot.

Disdained by his pupil, the tutor had disappeared for a few seconds, came back with a carbine, took aim, fired and shot the grey dolphin whose blood soon reddened the sea. The wonderful ballet ended in anguish and panic. Those clowns, those sea-angels rather, surrounded their wounded fellow and held her up. One of them tried to plug the gaping wound while another got snout to snout with the victim as if to kiss her, but in fact attempted to revive her with a type of mouth-to-mouth resuscitation; their whistling marked the rhythm of this artificial respiration. The pained scene receded on the waves. And then? Then Choutou-mounou seized the murderer and hurled him overboard.

Stupefaction was followed by wild activity; rings were flung overboard, the lifeboat launched, the tutor fished from the jaws of a shark that had arrived on the scene, attracted by the dolphin's blood.

The enraged captain advanced on Chou armed with a whip as long as a rattlesnake. A thick blind brute.

Then, Choutoumounou 'saw' flaming slavers being boarded by men brandishing axes, sabres and cutlasses, while O'O the Corsair gave them his blessing and urged them on from the mast.

'O'O! . . . O'O! . . .'

Blind fury in the purity of combat.

From the mainmast top and vast as the sea, that ancestral voice filled the sails of the ship and blew on the embers of the heart which quickened his flesh; it drove him irresistibly into action just as Greek gods goaded their heroes into the fray, assuring them of unfailing protection and saving them from the vengeance of other gods, magnifying the mortal fight and raising the conqueror to universal dimensions.

Forgetting mother and father, the family tie with the man

threatening him with the slave whip, eager and submissive to the voice from the sky, Choutoumounou struck.

Baingue! . . . Dingue! . . . Dingue!

The blood streamed. His skull fractured by a triple blow to the head, the captain was laid out on the bridge before he had even raised his arm to punish his nephew.

'*Aïe!* . . . *bon Dié* . . .' croaked an old sailor, '*mi mô!*' (He's dead!)

'*Tut moune ka mô ion jou,*' said another. (Everyone has to die one day.)

'*Thwo pwésé pa ka fè jou ouvè.*' (You speak too soon to rejoice at the captain's death.)

And again: '*Cap'taine là yo pov ti-bitin!*' (He's worth nothing anyway!)

'*Ki kè viv, kè wé* . . . (Who lives will see.)

As it happened, the captain, who heard the name O'O invoked on his schooner, was only wounded on the forehead by his nephew; but from then on he was known as 'Tibitin Baindingue' or Baindingue the Lesser throughout the Caribbean.

When both victims, groggy captain and half-drowned tutor had been tended to, and a time had been spent devising punishments, they looked for the culprit.

But Choutoumounou was not to be found. Without losing a moment, he had leapt into the boat used to rescue the tutor and still afloat on the sea, cut loose the mooring ropes and rowed away.

There he was on the high seas in the most dangerous pocket of the Caribbean where no sailor ventures without an intimate knowledge of winds and currents.

The terrible strait between Dominica and Martinique has not changed: in the same place, Christopher Columbus saw his fleet, made up of the flagship *Captain* and three others — the *Saint James of Palos*, the *Galician* and the *Biscay* — dispersed along the four cardinal axes of the compass, which effectively destroyed his plans to put in at Madinina island, otherwise known as Martinique.

To avoid attracting attention, Chou drifted for a while and was drawn rapidly out to sea. But he was a canny navigator and soon had the mast up and the little landing-sail kept to hand in case of storms hoisted — storms are frequent events in the tropical zone. Once at the helm, he tacked about and made for the shelter of Dominica. In the distance now, seen against the perpetually clouded peak of Pelée, Captain Tibitin Baindingue's schooner was transformed in the keen orange and greens of twilight into a ghost ship.

Skill saved Chou from the current that drives towards Saint-Pierre-et-Miquelon. He drew near the jagged emerald coastline as the glancing sunrays startled the valleys of sugar-cane into colour. He climbed a spar of lava in the sea and plunged his laughing face into the phosphorescent spray. A round mountainous form drew this comment from him:

'*Ouais! . . . à kay nous, ça plus belle!*' (Home — meaning Guadeloupe — is lovelier than this!)

All day he sailed on, rejecting the chance to put in for the night at Hwozo — Roseau — the capital of Dominica; instead he made straight for Sainte-Anne. He did not plan to stop at any of the Saintes, or at nearby Marie-Galante, for at Sainte-Anne he would be reunited with Pampou and there, too, he would explain everything to his father.

But if certain gods protect, others lay snares and ambushes that cut men down to size.

Seized with fear, the birds seemed to swim now rather than to fly. 'A bad sign,' thought Chou.

Clouds massed, and the four winds, unruly companions of Poseidon, came screaming in. Euros, who sang soft a moment earlier, unleashed itself against Zephyrus, who is usually gentle too, but holds murderous reserves of strength. Next, Notus and Borealis hurled themselves on their prey, the one with its hot blast, the other with its icy tongue; and the dance began, a dance in which each must dominate the other, bracing, losing ground, returning to the attack with renewed fury, combining their efforts, obeying the tragic idea.

Night deepened as the cyclone hit. The spinning motion seemed to draw hellward. The fragile boat was unmasted in a moment, and a huge wave broke on Choutoumounou who clutched on in desperation. Winds like a butting ram tried his grip, but he knew his life depended on holding tight. He wound his arms and legs around the boom, clamped a loose end of rope between his teeth, then grabbed another that looked stronger. At times he stiffened, at others relaxed his body and let it move with the violent oscillations of the current. He shifted a foot to ease cramp, and as he did so bit even harder on the rope; if he let go with his teeth he hugged the boat, looking for the tiniest toehold. Knocked flying, he seized hold again, groaning. Submerged, he held his breath. The roaming tornado whirled upon itself and hollowed out a space in the sea into which Choutoumounou emptied his stomach of salt water. The force returned with a siren's scream, and he screamed back to drown it out. The hollow was getting deeper.

Then the boat began to crack and cry out, as if begging him to release his grip. 'I'm lost,' thought Chou. 'The hull is going to break up and the sharks will have me. If Pampou were here we could defend ourselves from them by fighting back to back.

'I'll never let you go, scab! Do you want to see me dead you bitch! Whore! I'll hold on to you until you're smashed to pieces! I'm Choutoumounou, Holô King! If Pampou were here there'd be no talk of abandoning me — we'd talk of tearing you to pieces instead, and find a way out between two waves. But where *is* Pampou?

'O'O!' screamed the flailing boy.

No answer. Nothing but lightning, thunder, apocalypse. Were the ancestors resolved to let him die? There came a noise through the black cyclone, a sinister explosion.

And the Holô King felt himself lifted up. He was flung straight out of the water and then caught on the back of a long and lovely form, astraddle a marvellous body with a pectoral fin shaped like a sickle, whose skin was softer than silk. Despite his panic, the storm had grown so violent now that Chou thought only of losing himself in this softness. He embraced the long form as he might have embraced a woman, hugging it to him, wrapping his arms and legs around its muscles that seemed to respond to his every pressure. May that same softness not let him slip! Holding hard here, groping there, using his teeth, biting and sucking, he managed to cling close to his prey and was launched, body to body, through the appalling waves. The strange being below him whimpered gently and let out little throaty cries that seemed to urge him to tighten his grip as it leapt from wave to wave, plunging through the highest of them and resurfacing in shivers. The closer his embrace, the more triumphant the movements of the animal became. A siren! No, a woman, a real woman . . . the creature of his dreams, the very one he had embraced for those few instants during that famous boarding. It was Claire Gostze! He summoned her before his eyes. Who else should it be? It was unthinkable that she wouldn't come and save him after all that had happened between them. With that wild adventure their great love had begun. She wouldn't abandon him now, now that she had come to his rescue. But the storm grew more violent still, and he despaired of holding her in his arms for long; and yet, as soon as she felt him loosen his grip she slowed enough to make him regain courage and hold fast. Only lovers know that kind of effusion and intimacy. So Chou caressed Claire, and Claire sang for joy through the fearful howlings of the cyclone. He was swept away in all the revelation of that languorous body between his legs. He had the impression that as he trembled the body beneath him trembled too.

Strange, intoxicating experience for a boy, to find a woman giving way in his arms. And he too gave way. He didn't understand what was happening to him: he came.

There was lightning everywhere; when had the flashes been so brilliant, the air louder, the sea angrier?

It was revelation, ecstasy, this sudden explosion like a burst of thunder.

Dear God, what sweetness! Was it sea or woman that so licked his sides? The prelude to death? Then how gentle death is, how beautiful, how winning its golden aura!

O'O! . . . To die like this in the tempest!

From all sides the blows came raining down. Notus warmed his breath, then handed him over to Borus who froze his heart; Euros struck him with rapid blows that sent him reeling, entwined with his mistress, into the arms of Zephyr who welcomed him, snaring him in his wildly scattered hair. He was hot and cold by turns, shivering in the fury, but he never once let go the tender living form who urged him to keep hold of her slippery flesh with lascivious little chirps.

Thus, astraddle a dolphin that came to his aid, Choutoumounou was ferried in all directions through the Caribbean. He thought he held the woman of his dreams and caressed the dolphin which cried out with pleasure.

It is hardly surprising that he, like Pampou, lost all sense of time.

WHEN the news of Choutoumounou's disappearance at sea reached Vallet, Anne de Lériv thought she would go mad.

While the news was of Pampou, that scamp she began to find lovable, with his supposed amorous exploits which she laughed at secretly, she hadn't really resented her husband's decisions; she hadn't energetically opposed them, in any case. But the thought of Chou, her favourite, in danger, swept off by a cyclone, set her heart beating wildly. She became feverish. Nothing in her could accept that her child had been abandoned like that. All the passion and emotion she had repressed, with that peculiar skill for self-denial she had inherited from a long tradition that assigned women to the role of servants when even the slightest family decision had to be made, all this burst out with bitterness.

She attacked spiritedly: 'Who permitted you to strike my son with a slave-whip?' she asked her brother-in-law come shame-facedly to report the misfortune.

'Oh no! I never touched him!' Tibitin replied hastily, seeing that he was being accused of an enormous crime which in his slow-witted way he hadn't reflected upon. Now he was at pains to defend himself.

'Oh no, I jus' threatened!'

Having thus presented his case for the defence, visibly straining to express himself in French in deference to his 'white' sister-in-law, he breathed again, imagining himself absolved of guilt.

A black-treacle negro, Tibitin had been a sailor all his life. He treated his crewmen brutally, without pity. He had nothing to lose. On shore, he regularly frequented cafés and cabarets escorted by black buttocky prostitutes. He planted himself in a chair and sat through to the early hours tucking in to grilled cod and spicey onion, fat pork and black sausage, drinking punch and recounting the exploits of his ancestors as if he himself were the principal hero, while the assembled company of seaside negroes, longshoremen, sailors and other fornicators shook with dirty laughter; then the storyteller lashed out, sparking off a brawl. Before long he would

vomit his excess on to the floor. Still, Tibitin was prudent enough
to beware of Anne de Lériv, this inexplicable white, who passed for
his sister and sister-in-law, with whom he had played Holô and
fencing in years gone by. He had confusing recollections of her, and
as she confronted him now, fear dried out his mouth.

'So, you threaten a child with a slave-whip, then you throw him
into the sea!' shouted Anne de Lériv.

'No, no, that's not quite it,' Tibitin continued, groping
desperately for words. 'It was him, I mean Choutoumounou, who
chucked his teacher overboard!'

'So who, sir, left my son to the tempest? Which of you was
coward enough to abandon a child on the raging sea?'

'Didn't abandon Choumoune . . .'

'What's that? Of those on the ship did a single man go to his aid?
Not even you, captain and master of the ship!'

'Choumoune skedaddled, zoom!'

'But what did you do to get him back?'

'Cyclone hit, an' I beat it to Saint-Pierre . . .'

(He was lying; the cyclone hit later.)

'Now tell me, what did you do in port?'

'A long night!'

'By all means let them believe the night was long, though you're
not the type to spend it in reflection. But what sort of night did my
son spend, if he had one at all?'

'Calm again, we went from place to place; made for Hwozo,
Mai-Galante, the Saintes: nothin'!'

'What do you mean, nothing?'

'May I question him; after all, my interest is the same as yours?'
Baindingue interrupted. He feared his brother might let slip
something to reveal his cowardice.

'Shut up! Do you want me to die?' shouted the mother.

'But look here . . .'

'He said he saw nothing!' the poor woman continued, almost in
tears.

'Ach! If ah'd caught the lil' devil I'd of scoffed 'im!' said Tibitin
tactlessly.

'God! He wanted to catch my son to eat him!'

'I did'n say dat!'

'So what do you mean to say? First you strike my son with a

slave-whip, then you fling him into the sea, and as huge waves sweep him away, you make full speed for port to spend a snug philosophical night. And it would have to be Saint-Pierre, one of the most sordid ports in the Antilles!'

'Now, now,' Baindingue tried to come in and put a bit of order into this meaningless dialogue between his wife and brother; 'Now, my dear friend, let's try and examine the case closely without getting carried away. First of all, Choutoumounou is used to the sea, and the current might have carried him towards Saint-Christophe or Antigua, or even San Domingo. And please note that he was neither struck nor thrown overboard as by catachresis of interpretation you seem so sure is the case in your heart and mind.'

'God, how you irritate me, you two, with your different ways of talking! I want to know what's happened to my son, while you two just make sentences. He talks a frightful mixture of French and Creole, and you a stew of linguistic catachresis!'

'I beg you, Madame, calm yourself! It is prudent to warn you that nothing will come of this hysteria. I repeat: *primo*, your son was not thrown overboard; *secundo*, he flung his teacher overboard; *tertio*, he struck his uncle and, finally, *quarto*, he escaped in a boat. Those are the facts, nothing but the facts. Insist on them.'

'You put all the blame on him! You're like your brother, not out to help my son at all, but to capture him! Capture a child lost in the storm. . . . With what sauce would you like to eat the innocent, Lord Magistrate?'

'The boy's no longer a child, still less an innocent, you must agree. He deserves to be judged. After all, by throwing someone into the sea he perpetrated a crime punishable by law. So deliver him up to me for justice. This honourable teacher, whom I count among my friends, only just escaped from the sharks or so I'm told by more than one witness. He too will entrust me with the handling of this — delicate case. In the circumstances, I'm a better judge than anyone, and I've never done anything but cleave to the truth, whatever it is and whatever the results! The truth, the whole truth and nothing but the truth!'

'Sir! If you please, my son is lost at sea and all you think about is taking him to court!. A fine opportunity for you to preside over a trial where love and duty are at odds. Allow me to say that you are

a magistrate with a murderer's head! And your brother's a coward.
As for him, teacher and friend no less, he's a hired assassin!'

The teacher said nothing. Usually so gentle and well-mannered,
full of that characteristic Creole grace, this woman showed herself
in a different light: ardent, outraged, aggressive and disturbing.
What a fuss for a drowned nigger!

'I've been told, Madame,' said Baindingue, 'that you were once
a little . . . a little . . . ?'

'Say it then! A little mad . . . with people like you around, it's
easy!'

'Now, now my friend, I understand your distress, I understand
your grief and confusion; but you are getting swept away towards
an abyss . . .'

'I want to know who killed my son! If it wasn't you, and if it
wasn't your brother, then it must have been him!' And she pointed
a terrible accusing finger at the tutor. 'Oh God, what am I to
believe?' she cried in desperation.

'But Madame,' the tutor interjected unwisely, 'but Madame,
how my fault? What? I shoot a dolphin, then I'm seized, beaten
senseless and flung to the deeps: and all for a dead *cetacea*!'

'A gallant exploit, sir, to kill without being attacked, without so
much as the excuse of hunger! Do you get a retrospective thrill out
of it? Do your guts quiver from top to bottom in memory of that
glorious deed? So, you kill for the pleasure of it. Watching the flow
of blood is your favourite pastime and, what's more, to contemplate that blood disperse in dazzling clouds through the clear
waves and depths of the sea, mixed with all the thrills of cruelty
that you treasure, and to discover a palette infinitely nuanced,
makes you yelp with pleasure! Know then, sir, that by some
devilish urge your fine intelligence led you into the stupid act of
slaughtering a mammal not only inoffensive but particularly
sociable and useful. In your universal wisdom, do you not know
that these *cetacea*, as you call them, talk to sailors in a language that
is neither Greek nor Latin, but which touches the heart? The
miraculous sympathy between the two quite different species has
often led one to save the other in distress; the dolphin always saves
the victim of shipwreck from hungry sharks. And men have
banned shooting dolphins and undertaken in good conscience to
wage war on those that do kill them. Now you, you wretch, have

broken that pact. Your pointless crime condemns my son to death without mercy; lost in the storm, no dolphin will come to his aid until the one you slaughtered has been avenged! I shall avenge the dolphin, and my son! Ah! Ah! Ah! . . . I'll have you yet, by O'O! Ah! Ah . . . Ah!'

'My God! She's gone mad,' cried Baindingue.

The implacable 'madwoman', pathetic, ridiculous, insulting and threatening all at once, advanced on Tibitin who retreated towards the wall where the seascapes hung. It was as though the spineless long-distance captain wanted to put himself under the protection of one of those canvasses, a boarding scene in which men leapt like cats through the rigging, brandishing swords and pistols. He imagined she was going to come alongside him, broadside style, and he invoked the protection of masts, ropes, sails, even imaginary seas. He drew back, burning with embarrassment. He tried to hide, but where? He couldn't find protection in a canvas, however vivid.

The lunatic kept coming. Would she really strike?

'Ah! . . . Ah! . . . Ah! . . . My jolly captain, you're a hero of the Caribbean sea, and in a moment we'll award you our lifesaver's medal!'

She sprang, then dropped her shoulders.

'And you, Chief Magistrate, sir,' — she had changed tack — 'accomplice in this and many other crimes, such as trying to shut me up in a madhouse so you could get your hands on Durivage. Ah! Ah! Ah! . . . A wrecker who would profiteer from the war, laying hold on my inheritance?'

Her supple body bent forward from the waist, she moved to and fro between them, her hips moving, even when she stopped to chide one and then the other. She scorched them with her eyes, bared her teeth; her cheeks became hollow, she flared her nostrils and narrowed her gaze.

'And since I'm insane, Monsieur Fouquet-Tinville,' she turned menacingly to Baindingue, 'let's talk a little about my son's education, since you pretend I don't care about it, and examine your pedagogical methods: nothing but savagery, branding your own children's brows with razor cuts! That was how slavers marked out their captive African princes. And as for you, captain *Linngwez* (long-whip), you chose to go smuggle rum and tobacco rather than help a child in danger! Since the war broke out in Europe you've really forged ahead, the second Corsair of the Caribbean sea, trafficking from island to island, selling dear in one place, very dear, what you steal from somewhere else! I know about your petty swindling; it would make your ancestors sick to the very soul. Their ideals were never fraud or murder! Ah! Ah! . . . You had to get to Saint-Pierre double quick to be rid of your stinking cargo, my "Capitaine", whose lucrative deals (and what a business!) are sanctioned and shared by this honourable magistrate with his chief clerk here, the Professor of False Sciences!'

This was the trigger of the calamity.

'O'O! . . .' gasped Baindingue, 'the shit-stirrer, it's too much!'

Enraged, he advanced on her. He raised his arm to seize her; though his long years in Paris had dulled the sense of danger before the daughter of Marie de Lèriv, he could listen to no more.

He was only just in range when, with speed and precision she whipped a switch from the folds of her skirt, the switch fashioned by Tonton-Hubé, and with a flourish opened a wound in the middle of her husband's forehead, branding him as he had branded his children. Then, springing and feinting to left and right, lunge after lunge, her hand darting to and fro like the tongue of a snake, she blinded first Tibitin and then the tutor: their right eyes whipped clean out, gone forever! Amid the stridency of her vengeance, screaming as if she herself were the victim, she fled, and her crinkly hair, like fibres loosed from the silk-cotton-tree and blown by the east wind, burst into luminous crests.

ANNE DE LÉRIV was generally considered a Creole, with what that suggests of indolence, grace and seductive power. At first sight, indeed, she looked pure Creole. But her slanted eyes, set in deep sockets which shaded them from the sun, and her skin with the satiny sheen of a ripe fruit, suggested mixed blood — without telling whether she was cross-bred or mameluke, the issue of white and either quadroon or mulatto. Even her hair, with its mass of reddish curls, smacked of the sun.

What were the actual origins of this strange, troubling beauty?

It was generally said that her father was killed in a duel. No one had ever seen the man; he couldn't have been Saint-Houël, since he did not know Marie de Lériv was pregnant when he had tried to snatch her away from Vallet and marry her himself; he would not have tried had he known Marie was already to be a mother.

The general wisdom was that only a white would have been brazen enough to seduce Countess Marie de Lériv, daughter of the most famous Béké in the country, and thus Anne de Lériv was a true Creole, not in the vulgar sense of 'native', but in its unequivocal French meaning — a European born in the American colonies. And yet, if she really was a Creole in the strict sense, how could those reddish, ripening mango tints in her skin be explained? Likewise the hues curiously like the juicy fruit of the marmalade-tree — except by admitting some blood that was neither coolie, African, Chinese or European, but the issue of some odd combination of every race in the Caribbean melting-pot? The French use of the word Creole is in fact Reunionist, very much of the 1830s. In Guadeloupe as in Martinique, Creole[1] includes the whole range of colour, from pure white through to ebony, even if the Creole who is a little fairer than the rest considers herself the very fruit of Venus. Anne de Lériv was a true Creole in this sense, sprung from

---

[1] It should be noted here that in the Spanish Academy dictionary, for the word *criollo* (Creole etymology: *criar*, from the Latin *creare*) one finds: Applied to a negro born in America, as opposed to one who was brought from Africa.

another Creole who, at least in her youth, had been a Venus; her soul had been formed by a negro with green eyes, O'Dingue, and a mulatto with red eyes, Tonton-Hubé, her adoptive fathers.

If the striking light in her clear blue eyes that sometimes changed to sea-green invited contemplation, sending a shiver down the spine, melting the observer's flesh as a flame melts a candle, sometimes her clouded pupils revealed moist depths in which, among fugitive sparks, beyond any colour, was a deepening storm. During her nervous attacks she showed herself, at bottom, to be wild rather than repressed. She was married to the most dignified and learned negro in Sainte-Anne, a Chief Magistrate no less, and she lived in a room that was something like a gorgeous frame of which she was the centre. Nothing was denied her; her maids brought her whatever she coveted from the shops in Pointe-à-Pitre and presented them ceremoniously in the name of 'Missie Président'. But in spite of all these attentions, or perhaps because of them, she sometimes slammed the door, jumped on her horse and galloped along the tide-line. She would cross the fields of Vallet from grove to grove and head for the Grands-Fonds where she took refuge in Tonton-Hubé's hut, built not far from her mother's tomb.

Streaming with sweat, a prey to feverish agitation, she arrived like a whirlwind, intruding into the very heart of the old 'Commander's' retreat. She flung herself trembling into his arms, mad with being so deliciously overwrought, moaning at what she had had to endure 'down there', within the walls of her prison, the great plantation house.

He was her Tonton, hers alone and no one but hers! She would throw herself upon his chest and bury her face in his mane. And the witch-doctor, who had become more and more of a magician with age, consoled her, affectionately stroking her forehead, delicately rearranging her hair, lifting a fringe, replacing a lock, combing it back with his fingers to reveal her lovely eyes which were neither blue nor green but contained all those tints within them. Then, with great care, he lifted her up like a fragile object and laid her down on a mattress. Next, he brewed a strong tisane which he gave her to drink, while he rubbed her feet and hands with aromatic leaves, crushed and salted. Refreshed and revived, she was soon calm again. Then he would teach her how to free her spirit from earthly things by holding her breath three times in succession until she felt the beginning of asphyxiation. Then she was to invoke the person central to her passion or hatred, 'sweet vertiginous appeasement'.

Thus in the complicit tropical night, while the sky pulsed with many stars and the winds dared not disturb a single leaf in the forest for fear of interrupting, far from malicious eyes and venomous gossip tongues, side by side on the bare earth, his hand in hers, the sorcerer unfolded the O'O legend once again, in tones soothing to the spirit:

'Once upon a time, O'O tacked through the Caribbean on his sloop. He had succeeded in taming the dolphins, and now they showed him the route followed by the slavers.

'These marvellous fish, emitting small, almost human cries, were seized with compassion for the rebellious negroes who were flung to hungry sharks without a moment's hesitation. In single file, these 'sea-geese' bore down on the man-eaters, dispersed them and saved some of the wretched slaves, while the speediest swam off in search of O'O.

'O'O's sloop sped across the waters:

'O'O!. . . O'O!. . .

'O'O's sloop bucked, leapt and sang on the sea:

'O'O!. . . O'O!. . .

'The breeze bellying out the sails swallowed up the distance.

'A soft voice from the sea cried out: .

'O'O!. . .'

'It was a little negress, borne aloft by a dolphin and calling for help.

'O'O raced on, saved her and became her companion . . .'

HAVING branded her husband and in two smart lunges blinded Tibitin and the Professor of False Sciences, Anne de Lériv of course made straight for Tonton-Hubé's cabin.

She was deeply distraught; had she been stronger she would have murdered those three monsters. For her, nothing existed but her sons. Her shoulders convulsed and she grew paler than moonlight on the sea.

She didn't even take her Arab pony — the idea didn't cross her mind — and instead went on foot towards the Grands-Fonds.

She rushed across the lawns of Vallet. The blue flame-tree watched her go without a flicker; it too was part of a great conspiracy. Judging her direction, it divined there was something in the air. Having reached the woods she stamped down brambles and pushed her way through the acacias, drove on through a cane-field, her face scratched by the tall plumes that tried to arrest her and stifle her with pollen. Her anguish was too great; she did not have the courage simply to lie down and die.

As night fell, the last rays of the sun went in pursuit, projecting her enormous shadow on to the swaying shadows of the plantation. A freshness seemed to emanate from the marshes in this vicinity. When she stopped by one of them to get her breath, she heard the murmur of the wind and the cackle of a moorhen, followed by the distant hooting of an owl, abruptly swallowed up in the thicket. She was overcome by its call. Chou's handsome face, which she had summoned with such intensity, appeared in her imagination as if bursting out of a pod. Her heart contracted as she thought she saw him submerged beneath gigantic waves and carried off by a whirlwind, turning and turning in the water, screaming for help, with only his widened eyes visible in the storm, his cries lost in the vast plantation. Maddened by this vision, she skirted the pool of lapping water and ran on, exalted and borne beyond her normal strength. It was as though she ran on pillows of rising mist, now wreathed in white gauze, now appearing like a torch. Those who saw her pass crossed themselves, thinking she was the Guiablesse, flying to Tonton-Hubé.

Some whispered behind their hands that her visits to Tonton-Hubé were not entirely innocent, and called her 'Mam'-Hubé' or 'Madame Hubert', while others went so far as to brand her the 'mulatto's mistress'. Everyone thought the worst of her, since she was neither white, black or mulatto but red! And as for Tonton-Hubé with his . . .

. . . She fell headlong into a ditch, got up painfully, struggled towards the Grands-Fonds, her hair flying and her eyes haggard. Fireflies winked around her.

Just as she was going to collapse, perhaps for the last time, an ancient fair-haired giant on a galloping horse caught her up, and without stopping placed her on his saddle in front of him where he held her tightly with his arm. He looked at her strangely out of empty sockets, and smiled with his fleshless jaws, as though rejoicing to have found her.

Their gallop went on through the forest until they arrived at Tonton-Hubé's cabin where he put her down and vanished, crying 'O'O! . . .'

How did she get there?

And who took pity on her?

Clutching both hands to her chest, her mouth wide and gasping for breath, she staggered into Tonton's hut.

What she saw, despite her blurred vision, felled her: she collapsed, fainting, into the arms of her sons.

For there they were.

There they were, both of them, Chou and Pampou. Along with Tonton-Hubé, they had been waiting for her. They were sitting down to a *blaff*, a fish soup with green bananas, bread-fruit, yams and rum, waiting for their mother. And they were speaking Creole, eating Creole, drinking Creole.

Chou had been recounting how the grey dolphin, the beautiful, long and languorous female — wounded by that flabby tutor, that wretched, ignorant, bestial and corrupt worm — had been saved by her fellow dolphins and had come to his rescue: 'O fearful night, braced against the cyclone! O blessed relief when, like a second cyclone, that marvellous creature appeared ! . . .'

After the tempest had died down, she took him on a journey

round the whole Antillean crescent, and promised him that one day she would follow the route taken by O'O the Buccaneer across the Atlantic to Africa, in search of his ancestors; she would take him as far as the Mediterranean and on into the Aegean to discover the Cyclades, those famous Greek islands that circle round Delos with their sonorous evocative names: Kéos, Kinthos, Sériphos, Siphnos, Milo — its beaches cradled Aphrodite — Sikinos, Amorgos — homeland of Simonides, where they make the costly flower-painted tunics; Naxos, where Ariadne lamented along the desolate beaches; Paros full of marble and sculptors; Syros, Mykonos, stony Delos where Apollo's golden palm rose above teeming palaces and sanctuaries; Tinos, Andros, Théra, with its harbour of boiling, sulphurous water and its cliffs that tower over the hollows of extinct craters. . . . Luminous lands indeed, but bitter ones. They pale before the Caribbean islands, more luminous with their luxuriant vegetation and miraculous waters, their dazzling beaches washed by a sea with a thousand tones and faces.

Those who neglect the Caribbean will retain a serious ignorance!

How clever she was at nosing out the best-sheltered harbours where she taught him to play the most sophisticated form of Holô; this consists not only in leaping out of the water to escape the shark's jaws, but also in clinging on to his singing companion. He could do anything with her. Through love she turned as white as Claire!

Pampou was all ears. That the beach at Sainte-Anne should be a trollop was scarcely surprising since it was used by all the bathers; but for a dolphin to become a woman? This was matter indeed. He admitted that his brother's amorous exploits matched his own, and he looked up to him as a brave and experienced guide as far as love was concerned. The dolphin became their common property. But how to make love to a dolphin?

Tonton-Hubé smiled, his eyes flashing as he remembered. He knew. He had often watched the dolphins swim past Vallet and recognized the grey one, the most beautiful of all the females, for she was graceful and voluptuous. She was O'O's little negress, coloured like the acajou. From his earliest childhood he had loved her tenderly, and would do so to the end of his days. She was the only mistress he had ever had, and though he continued to love her, he ceded her gracefully to the Little Twins.

Choutoumounou said he wanted to stay with her and discover the world: but a mysterious signal flashed, the sky turned a deeper blue, taking them by surprise on a beach of the Désirade. In obedience to a will greater than her own, 'Delphinus' put an end to their play and ferried him back to Sainte-Anne.

At this point in his story, Anne de Lériv staggered into the bamboo cabin.

Although Tonton-Hubé had assured them she wouldn't be long in coming, and they passed the time telling each other their tales, embellishing here and there, nothing could have moved them more than her dramatic entrance.

'What she must have been through!' the old man exclaimed to himself when he saw the state she was in. 'Something must be done, and quickly.'

The seventy-year-old looked young and sprightly, his eyes shining and that unshakable faith in the future emanating from his person.

No sooner thought than done: a cinnamon grog, mixed with a generous dash of rum, already steamed. He tended to her with such tender delicacy that her nightmare was soon forgotten. Fear, danger and remorse no longer held her, and in this recovery she proved clearly her mother's daughter.

That evening in the bamboo cabin they sang and danced the 'Toum-Black', the most powerful rhythm that Marie de Lériv had put to music, based on an old slave-song.

Tonton-Hubé began in his beautiful baritone:

O Silingue!
O Baindindingue!
O Silingua? . . .

(Where are you, Baindindingue, where are you?)

An invisible spirit answered, intoning the same call and drawing out the last syllable:

O Silingue!
O Baindindingue!
O Silinguâ . . . â . . . â . . . ?

Chou and Pampou sang in chorus:

Ah! Kalaïe

Baindindindingue, O'Silingua . . .
Ah! Kalaïe,
Baindingue, O'Silinguo! . . .
(I am here, Baindindingue, it is I!)
Anne de Lériv had quickly recovered her senses; she joined in
and sang in her gentle soprano the slaves' lament after capture:
Moin pôve nègue
Io Kimbé
Io marré
Io lié
Ah! Kalaïe
Baindindingue O'Silingua
Ah! Kalaïe
Baindindingue O'Silinguo! . . .
(Poor captured negro, held and bound; ah! Baindindingue,
deliver me!)
The woman sang and danced with the boys, improvising other
words — first the captured negress who is bound, and then the
mother separated from her children — while Tonton-Hubé played
the tom-tom.
Tall, slim, still beautiful despite her weariness, Anne swayed
from side to side, holding her skirt up delicately with one hand. A
glimpse of her naked leg . . .
The twins surrounded their mother, singing and dancing, and
started to re-enact a capture:
'O'O! . . .
'*Io Kimbé! . . . Io marré! . . . Io lié*!! . . .
One held the other, and bound him to the quickening rhythm.
Toum-Black! went the tom-tom at each stage.
Then the whipping scene: the one who received the biting
strokes from the imaginary whip convulsed, writhed, twisted,
glistening as the thong itself would glisten.
These two savages, convulsed, sent ripples through the air.

> The tom-tom beats it, out.
> The frenzied rhythm comes in waves,
> The intense, inevitable,
> Bewitching of the body.

Suddenly, the victim manages to free himself, to slay his torturer and to flee, to the sound of the tom-tom!

But now the three of them were acting out the 'boarding' of a woman. The liberated slave seeks a woman. She welcomes him with loving movements . . .

Anne shivered with tenderness at the voluptuous contact with her sons. What a pleasurable game! She believed a mother should give herself up to such excess. Her sons were now men; what whirlwind lay in wait for them? Her eyes gleamed — she was ready for anything. With her supple, muscular hips moving rhythmically she offered herself, withdrew and enveloped the young males — more eager even than she — until they came together.

Toum-Black! went the tom-tom.

Choutoumounou in front, Pampou behind, the twins imprisoned their prey, keeping time to the rhythm. Anne gave herself, a marvellous offering to her sons. Raising her arms, she placed her hands on the nape of her neck and tousled her fiery hair; her raised elbows afforded a glimpse of the red hair under her arms. She could not release herself fast enough.

She came forward, drew back, made contact . . .

Toum-Black!

At every beat a sensual wave swept over her, she tensed and relaxed to the rhythm. Confusion in her thighs, in the firm curves of her hips. She thrust out her hips, her whole body shivered. Now she stretched her arms before her, threw back her head provocatively. Now her shoulders trembled, she thrust her breasts forward; everything took form in her supreme audacity. The open-mouthed pleasure of the young lovers. The mother gives birth; it is she who must teach sexuality, the one creative source in life, to be honoured and respected. The most solemn religious act is that of fertilization, and only the mother can be fertilized; it is she who receives. For this she must give herself, and in doing so she gives everything. The mother danced, with her belly, her pelvis, her buttocks — each in turn — and with her coucoune,[1] to teach her children sex. It is the lost meaning of the Toum-Black.

The boys' joy — how to describe it? Their solitary pleasures now became sublime.

Their mother gave, gave, gave.

---

[1] *Coucoune*: woman's sex; *foufoune*: female virgin's sex.

She was a divine offering, for nothing could be more of a gift than the initiating mother. Drunkenness, madness!

Her sons mimed the final intimacy in sacred movements. They understood that man was made for woman, woman for man. They entered the adult world and left their solitary pleasures behind. They renewed the vital chain.

The mysteries revealed to troubled spirits are exalting. Their bodies came and went in harmony with their breathing.

The old sorcerer, himself bewitched, went wild on the tom-tom.

When the earth gave way beneath them, the rhythm came faster, bodied out a second earth for them.

Everything affirmed this vital ritual. The rhythm transfigured deed, bridging the gap between impulse and act.

The old mulatto's eyes, sunk in his flushed face, were redder than ever; a strange smile played over his face.

On the last stroke of midnight came a piercing cry:

'O'O! . . .'

Even the silence hung in suspense.

On the veranda of the cabin, Marie de Lériv was seated before her open tomb. The tombstone looked like a piano, and she played the famous chords of the Toum-Black on a keyboard of clacking bones while a second spectre, Count de Lériv, her tall and fleshless father, wearing the Red Corsair's long hair for a shroud, with a violin tucked under his chin, played swinging improvisations on the slave song as he capered round the open grave that exuded a mouldering smell. The ghost leapt like a gazelle, drawing out the 'Io Kimbé . . . Io marré . . . Io liés' with great sweeps of his bow. Is buffoonery given to the dead?

In the barbarous darkness of the forest, adorned now with bats as a cathedral with gargoyles, the tropical wind caressed the cactus with its claws.

Cha! . . . cha! . . . cha! . . .

How resonant the night was; how laden with scent the air . . .

The zombies came up from hell at the call of the Toum-Black, and at the head of their haggard number marched the Big Twins, demanding the Law . . .

> Mysterious forest
> Big-boled and vast,

> In a grotesque convulsion
> Gives one enormous laugh . . .

How strange the road that leads to Liberty!

ONCE the Great War was over, Baindingue decided to send his sons to further their studies in Paris.

He had had more than enough of their escapades. They would have to be separated, above all from their mother, for he had heard too many terrible stories about their wild, equivocal dances with her night after night in Tonton-Hubé's cabin. Both mother and sons, he believed, were a little deranged. In Paris, Choutou-mounou and Pampou would be shaken into sense and saved. In addition, he planned to appoint a guardian to accompany them and supervise their activities.

He was determined to break them in, and break them in he would. His wife must be broken too. In that god-forsaken country his boys threatened to turn into loutish good-for-nothings who would tarnish his otherwise spotless reputation as a magistrate and man of integrity; it had shone even brighter since the Armistice. He and his brother Tibitin were officially credited with having kept Guadeloupe and Martinique supplied with flour for bread. It was Baindingue, Baindingue the magistrate, who conceived the plan of action and financed it out of his own pocket, while Tibitin his brother — that rugged sailor worthy of O'O the Buccaneer — dodged the surveillance system set up by German submarines blockading the Antilles. He mounted a boarding operation against a German supply ship, and in the ensuing struggle lost an eye . . . that, at least, was the official story. People had thought they were trafficking in rum and tobacco, but now the radiant truth shone out for all to see. The brothers were duly decorated with a thoroughly merited *Légion d'honneur*. People always like to believe stories about corrupt magistrates; it is only human nature to want to cast in doubt the integrity of men of law, especially when the detractors are totally lacking in personal integrity. Baindingue was a clever man.

Proud as peacocks, the decorated heroes led the Little Twins through the crowd and on to the quayside at Pointe-à-Pitre. The magistrate carried an ivory-topped cane and wore a bowler hat —

which was hard to distinguish from his ebony head. He was the incarnation of dignity and respectability. As for the sailor, he paraded in a new hat, adorned with the braid and insignia of Staff Captain. In one of his long ape-like arms he cradled the slave-whip — from which he was inseparable — and he glanced from left to right with his Cyclopean eye, ashamed of his affliction, and ready to punish the first urchin who dared so much as point it out. They were surrounded by other members of the Baindingue clan, brothers, half-brothers, cousins, in-laws and close family friends. They basked in the excitement that such departures for France always caused: all of them were dressed to the nines in a way ludicrously incompatible with the climate. Some even wore the felt hats that were the very latest fashion, while their wives, beautiful crinkly-haired negresses and mulattos, wore crinolines, tight corsets that displayed their firm busts to advantage, and all manner of jewellery and ornament. They took pleasure in being looked at, but woe to anyone with an ironic spirit, for they were vain too, and continually on the look-out.

They halted several times to make a general impression. Indeed, they did all they could to be seen. Parading together like this, they hoped to scotch stories circulating about their enormous wealth and the questions that lingered on about the real nature of their activities during the war, in the course of which only one O'O, who was blind drunk at the time, got himself killed in a dispute with the whites and consequently earned the name O'l'Eo (O'O the Hero) — a glory from which the clan drew considerable profit.

With Anne on his arm, Tonton-Hubé addressed the Little Twins who shifted sullenly from foot to foot.

'What does the whiteman's country hold in store for you, my poor little negroes?'

At which point Tibitin drawled:

'They'll be well and truly tanned!'

Anne stared intensely at the Cyclops: hadn't he learnt his lesson? Would she have to put out his other eye before he held her children in respect? Once more her sons were being torn from her — she might never see them again — and it was possibly all thanks to that old driveller.

It was clear she hadn't completely recovered her demeanour since the crisis. Her chest heaved with repressed anger. She tried to free her arm, but Tonton restrained her.

Pampou stiffened at his uncle's words. The young man, whose gaze scared even his parents, was already spoiling for a fight. So Tibitin had threatened his brother with a slave-whip? He would have murdered him for that, had he been there. And he had still to avenge his brother's being abandoned at sea. It was as well, therefore, to settle a few debts there and then on the quayside, so no one should forget Pampou. He had dreamed of such a confrontation.

Choutoumounou laid a hand on his brother's shoulder and smiled straight into the brutal face of his uncle Tibitin — more beastly than ever now, since his mother had put out his eye. Now he was trying to make his presence felt by fingering that terrible whip.

Did he really think that weapon frightened him, Choutoumounou? On the bridge of the schooner he had moved more rapidly than the old bloat-face; every weapon can fail if you count on it too much. Chou pretended not to notice the intended threat. Having seen the slave-whip waved to and fro in front of his nose, he knew quite well that any man who struck out with such a whip before such a crowd would be lynched. Added to that, Pampou was by his side, ready to take on one flank while he himself dealt with the other. He knew that the slightest pressure on his brother's shoulder would trigger an attack; their mother was there too, with her switch hidden in the folds of her skirt. Tibitin would lose his other eye if he took it into his head to raise the slave-whip.

Entertaining such thoughts, the fantastic boy looked past his uncle for his ex-tutor, the Professor of False Sciences, forgetting that he had fled Guadeloupe as if pursued by a demon. When he remembered that, Choutoumounou's smile became even wider, enough to make everyone wonder what he might be thinking. Had he become an idiot?'

None of this escaped Baindingue. He was the most learned of the O'O, and with his complex personality seemed the best equipped to succeed in all his projects. He had far-reaching ambitions. First, Choutoumounou and Pampou were to receive an education worthy of his own position, and for that it was necessary to send them to a great school in Paris. His sons must become lawyers, magistrates or doctors, and he would pay to see that they did.

Above all, it was essential they should leave the country, not only for their own good but to teach Tonton-Hubé, not to mention his own wife, that scandalous redhead, a lesson. He too had noticed quite a few things recently. As long as the old mulatto was alive and Anne de Lériv at liberty, he would be unable to get his hands on Durivage which, merged with Vallet, would make up the biggest agricultural complex in Guadeloupe. There were fabulous riches to be had, and he was a born calculator. The successful are those in whom a definite ambition gives shape to the soul and models their features; those who are called by their high destiny to climb the bitter summit, who walk pensively, preoccupied by a supreme goal; to adapt the words of Victor Hugo — frequenting teachers is no bad thing in itself. Then he could even become Deputy! That, in fact, was what this dispenser of justice wanted more than anything; for the Antillean negro it was the highest glory. To achieve it he would do anything. With his sons out of the way he would destroy Tonton-Hubé and neutralize his wife. If they refuse to change, then they must disappear. He could perhaps send a rogatory commission to furnish him with information about the notorious 'Nights in the Grands-Fonds'. They were nothing less than Bacchic rites, lubricated with rum, where even the Capesterre Indians came to perform their Shiva dances, not to mention the Haitian voodoo-men. It was all in a blameless cause, they said: encouraging the crops, harnessing supernatural forces, calling up the dead, investing themselves with ancestral powers and healing the sick. In Baindingue's opinion, they took advantage of these nocturnal gatherings to indulge in occult séances that quickly caught on among other groups and led to all manner of excess, from brawling to sordid orgies and group copulation. In short, these meetings, convened on the pretext of 'folk-dancing', were neither more nor less than an attempt to subvert public order and morals.

'Only introverts and extroverts find an outlet for their impotence on these occasions, and Monsignor Magloire certainly won't join the perpetrators to defend the "Lagghia" and the "Convalin"[1] and other forms of Toum-Black. They are nothing more than a regrettable relic of the savage's primitive mode of

---

[1] Antillean dance related to karate.

expression. And modern dance is nothing more than a resurgence of animality. If the body is unrestrained it becomes a puppet. The dispersal of internal energy in these demonic explosions fragments the personality. The primitive likes to carry on in defiance of all the laws of nature and runs the risk of losing his soul and his sense of the divine. The perversion begins with a rum punch, and ends in unchained sexuality, dionysiac madness and a blasphemous parody of the Passion and Resurrection. The people need Peace, Bread and Religion – P . . . B . . . R . . . ! If liberty is a great conquest for humanity, it must not be ridiculed by libertinism.'

This was how Baindingue, Chief Magistrate of Western Culture, reasoned with himself, with the whole Church behind him. He could imprison the old sorcerer and leave him to starve. He could shut his wife up in a madhouse and obtain an annulment of his marriage from Rome, which would leave him free to marry Claire Gostze, daughter of his old law teacher, and with a genuine white wife at his side he would win the Béké vote. He would be Deputy at last! This was how he reasoned privately, Baindingue, Chief Magistrate and Man of Integrity, trained in the schools of Paris. At what price, Deputy? He would take his seat in the Chamber. Then, he dreamed, something sublime must come to pass. He would be vice-president of the Chamber, who knows? President! And Minister in due course no doubt. 'If I was made Colonial Minister,' he thought, 'no one would dare raise a finger against me. If politics leads, as it always leads, to greater and greater power over the people, and if libertarians always try to oppose that tendency, it is still true that politics can adapt its judicial machinery to counter-attack, and sooner or later immorality will be stamped out by a system of multiple laws. I know the Law. And no one will dare raise a finger against me!'

Baindingue dreamed of his exalted future; the red-eyed mulatto watched him with an ironic smile on his lips. However pitiless and proud he expected Baindingue to be, he showed no sign of flinching. 'I may be your uncle,' thought the old man, giving himself away for the first time, 'but woe to you if you lay a finger on my daughter!'

Meanwhile, Chou and Pampou defied their uncle Tibitin; the prospect of ridiculing him still remained tempting.

This family seemed to lack any kind of moderation.

Then three whistle blasts interrupted the potential charm in that tense situation.

The sun sparkled on the water.

From their place in the very centre of the vivid crowd that chattered in sing-song Creole, they had to thread their way through and jump into the rowing-boat which slipped straight out on to the limpid surface of the sea, scarcely rippled by a warm breeze heavy with fragrance. Quite a flotilla already circled the big steamer *France* of the General Transatlantic Company. The customs officer went about in his small boat. They embarked.

'*Adieu Foulard, adieu Madras!* . . .' sang the crowd.[1]

Up on the bridge the Little Twins contemplated Karukéra: it swam like a living emerald between two arms of blue.

Mangroves were bathed in the soft sludge from the Arboussier factory. Here and there, canna, filaos and orchids rose up, masking the branches of other astonishing trees; flowering branches of vivid shrubs tangled with hanging and climbing plants, thick ferns and other teeming vegetable parasites. Mangos, laced together by clematis and convolvulus, made an impenetrable curtain. The breeze stirred the leaves until for all the world they seemed to be whispering. The volcanic hills rose and fell, and in the hazy distance blue valleys and blue hills surrounded blue peaks.

A magic island. Its mass flamed out as if enveloped in a rainbow veil that shot flakes of fire into the dazzling sky.

Facing this, the O'O twins felt great sadness well up in them, so strong they could no longer speak to each other. They were overcome by a chaos of feelings.

'What does the whiteman's country hold in store for you, my poor little negroes?' the old red-eyed mulatto had wondered to himself.

They were bowed down with what seemed the cares of the whole world.

'Will they see the Isles again?'

Their new adventure would no doubt be exciting; but would they see the Isles again?

Enormous scarlet clusters, planted along the shore, flared. And

---

[1] Strangely enough, the music for this Antillean hymn is by Jean-Baptiste Lully, the seventeenth-century Italian composer.

each purple flame-tree, the *Delonix Regia*, quivered like a cry of passion.

Suddenly the beach of Sainte-Anne, and then Vallet came into view. On the green lawn by the lake, there was the blue flame-tree, glowing bluer, bluer than even the distant hills. As though little blue bulbs were concealed in its foliage.

They felt sick in the pits of their stomachs. Their umbilical cords had been carefully sealed in an envelope woven of cane-cuttings, inscribed like a birth certificate, detailing the very hour of their arrival in the world. Then it had been locked away in a small steel box by their Indian grandmother, a Buddhist. When one of them died in a distant country, the other was to fetch his body and bury it under that tree. That was where they were born, that was where they would rest. There would always be an old negro or negress who, in memory of the Big Twins, would render the same service to the surviving Little Twin.

Chou and Pampou tried to persuade each other that they would both return, and that these heavy feelings were unimportant and would be soon forgotten.

'Leaving is nothing, so long as we have each other.'

Leaning against the rails, they drew closer. They shared the sad pleasure of feeling alone. The bitter-sweet melancholy that accompanies a major departure swelled up as the horizon receded. Despite his resolve, Pampou began to shake and his colour became as dark as the rail he clenched with his fingers.

And then, almost without being aware of it, the Little Twins began to cry. They cried with tenderness and grief, as one does when one has to leave home. It is sheer pain, and they were children who hadn't yet learned how to bear their griefs.

A school of dolphins arrived to console them, sea-foam glistening on their skins. There was a murmur of voices, mingled sounds from distant centuries; faint sounds coming through in a choral lament, like the blurred speech of the slaves. Was this the Ancestral Tide?

The grey-headed dolphin sped its frolicking movements, quick leaps in which the body seemed launched for the sky, then jack-knifed down, plunged into the depths, its will to live expressed in its ecstatic abandonment.

Flying fish streaked the sky.

Would they escape? Where might they fly?!

The Little Twins gulped the last warm gusts of the tropics.

Abruptly, the sun set in a wreath of yellow, blue and violet rays; then that famous ray of green, pure green.

Sky and sea became one.

Afterword

A recurrent obsession of Antillean literature is the re-exploration of the history of the islands — a history so long distorted by the folk-culture image created by the West. This historical research, or this appeal to the past, often takes the form of re-creating history by linguistic means, in an attempt to combat what the Martinique poet Edouard Glissant has called in *Le Discours Antillais*, 'the effacement of the collective memory'. A new Antillean mythology must be written, one purged of images conceived solely by and for the whites.

The same passionate desire informs very different works, depending on the personal sensibility and trajectory followed by each writer. In *The Blue Flame-Tree*, Jean-Louis Baghio'o uses historical facts in the manner of a traditional story-teller, weaving them into the heart of a fiction always rich and startling. In *Issandre the Mulatto*, one of his earliest works, Baghio'o already revealed himself to be both poet and story-teller, placing his characters in mystical but natural settings, his style feeding on the musical and lyrical tradition that gives his story its unique atmosphere.

The Blue Flame-Tree can be described as the saga of the O'O clan (the two last letters in the name Baghio'o). Narcissism pure and simple? Not at all, since it becomes clear that the O'O are a real presence in the historical and cultural complexity that constitutes the Antillean peoples. The family tree at the beginning of the story functions as the emblem of an historical continuum, of which for a long time the people themselves could have no notion, deprived as they were of their language and cultural inheritance. To remedy this, Jean-Louis Baghio'o undertakes to chronicle in his own way the lives of people official histories never mention. Following the fortunes of the O'O family, who began as pirates, slaves and runaways, we witness the rise of a new class, the land-owning mulatto bourgeoisie of the nineteenth century that came to rival their former white masters in power and influence. Some real courage and honesty is required of Baghio'o here, since Antillean literature has tended to be biased towards the oppressed, at the expense of the oppressor. His chosen characters are slaves, sugar-cane workers, sometimes rebels. For him, the world is riddled by class and racial prejudice. Yet he remains open to the redeeming violence of nonconformist elements, creating new models for himself. The O'O, for example, never forget the courage of their pirate-ancestor who stitched himself a pair of breeches from the skin of the unhappy whites who fell victims to one of his boarding operations. From father to son — and it's worth noting the author's fascination with twinship, which is a leitmotiv running through the book — name follows on from name like an echo of resistance coming down through the centuries and a rallying cry for those who were never subjugated. While the masculine line perpetuates the ferocious aspect and ebony skin of the O'O, the women introduce new blood into the family and form the very heart of the narrative. First, there is the Hindu Indian, so often omitted from Antillean literature. She is 'inventive in devotion, loving and caring, courageous and of millenarian faith', the archetype of the Oriental Mother. But the feminine character who dominates the centre of the stage, like the central hearth in a temple, through which everything is possible, contact and communion as well as fecund dispersal, is Marie de Lériv, descendant of the Red Corsair. Marie powerfully reverses the stock image of the pale and languid Creole. Refusing the hot-house existence which was the only role her society could offer her, she broke through the barriers that enclosed her insular world and went to live with the O'O, by then one of the most powerful black families in Guadeloupe. It is clear that Baghio'o wishes Marie to incarnate the Mother figure, and similarly in a later novel, *The White Hummingbird*, in the person of Fernande de Virel (anagram of de Lériv), the fabulous Creole mother is blessed with multiple artistic gifts. In this context, one is perhaps justified in suspecting Baghio'o of being too schematic in his treatment at times, and of using too liberally elements that make up the island 'adventure stories' he is at pains to condemn. But that is to be a pedant and a kill-joy. The story carries one away, both by its preternatural events and by its startling characters who constitute an arresting gallery.

Baghio'o's style helps us to plunge into a fantastically-coloured reality, so much so that in the end we ask which is the more extraordinary, the historical reference or the fictional inventiveness? This is an historical novel, even if the author interprets history imaginatively and subjectively, and as such the tension between what belongs properly to history and what to fiction has a crucial bearing on its final form. The form of *The Blue Flame-Tree* is linked to that of the narrative-epic, which explains its manifest tendency to parody, laughter and the postulation of a different image for man. To fuel his writing, Baghio'o makes the fullest possible use of the oral tradition while at the same time remaining anxious to impart his own personal information, explanations and interpretations. By setting the action in the past, outside the reader's experience, he creates a new kind of communication, founded nevertheless on traditional procedures. Because of this, the passages of dialogue are especially significant.

It must be made clear that readers whose taste is for a militant and didactic form of literature will be disconcerted, for *The Blue Flame-Tree* is something altogether different. They will find description that smacks of the exotic, and be astonished that the white man's life-style should be delineated with such seeming complicity. They will search in vain for the 'cause' espoused by the author. And yet they will not fail to be touched by his love for the Antilles, a love that is manifest in these pages. Equally, they will admit that the importance of the islands is rather magnified, and that many different, contrasting portraits can be made, depending on who is writing, from the diversity and complexity, the chequered histories and destinies of a place where so many peoples came together.

Finally, without presuming to intrude upon that privacy so precious to him, perhaps we can briefly outline the major events that have shaped Jean-Louis Baghio'o's career. As an engineer in radio broadcasting and the author of a number of technical works, he took an active part in organizing underground radio transmission during the German Occupation of France from 1940–45. After the war he was appointed Technical Director of French Broadcasting Overseas, and used the opportunity to attack, publicly and outspokenly, the colonialist policy of the period. He counted among his friends Leon-Gontran Damas of French Guyana and the President of Senegal, Léopold Sédar Senghor —

two of the great *poètes de la négritude* — and the Madagascan Rabemananjara, editor of *Présence Africaine*; in his own particular style he has joined them in paving the way for a new political awareness.

Maryse Condé